MASTER MERRYMAN

Carol Richards

ISBN-13: 978-1463625542

CONTENTS

Chapter One

Lambeth palace

Christmas 1497

It was the season of frost fairs and mistletoe.

Across the cold unforgiving river the twin towers of Westminster Abbey were shaded onto a leaden sky that held no promise of angels.

Nor as yet any sign of the company expected.

In Lambeth Palace, residence of His Grace the Archbishop of Canterbury (also Lord President of the Privy Council, Chancellor of the Exchequer and as Cardinal, the Pope's representative in England) all was hustle and bustle.

The Yule log had been dragged in and placed in the huge grate in the banqueting hall where it was left to smoulder.

By the time the feast got under way it would be well alight and there would be a roaring fire to greet the company which would be as illustrious as any in England outside the King's Court for the guests of honour were to be the Flemish and Spanish Ambassadors.

The maids were hanging boughs of holly and ivy from the rafters. Gilded pine cones and oranges spiked with cloves and cinnamon were placed in dishes along the tables.

A great salt, newly commissioned and magnificently wrought in silver gilt in the shape of a ship as like in miniature to the "*Matthew*" captained by Master Cabot that had lately landed in the New Found Land as the goldsmith's art could conceive was receiving a final polish before being given pride of place on High Table.

Among all this activity a slender young man could be seen adjusting this, criticizing that and ever and anon running to the tall perpendicular windows to see if *they* had at last arrived.

He was thirty-one years old, his hair nut-brown under a velvet cap. His eyes were nearer black.

He was handsome with fine-cut features and his figure, while a trifle thin reflecting the inroads made by his restless nervous nature was lithe and athletic.

He had a ready smile and a joke for anyone who had placed a decoration crookedly or laid the table incorrectly.

There was something easy in his manner that endeared him to his fellow servants although he had the management of them.

He was the Master of the Revels and his name was Henry Medwall.

Although he was for the occasion acting as Cardinal Morton's Steward that was not his true position in the household.

To be truthful no-one was quite certain what his position was for his presence was at times rather like that of a Will o' the Wisp. He came, he went, but no-one was ever quite sure where from or where to.

In the household accounts he was listed as the Cardinal's chaplain and indeed he had been ordained for seven years but there was not much of the priest about Henry Medwall.

He was dressed to be fair in clerical black but what priest took to the streets with a sword at his hip?

He was not wearing it now of course being indoors and about his duties.

All the same he was very well dressed.

He wore a white chemise of the finest linen which was fashionably short over black hose. His shirt was caught up in soft folds and kept in place by a gold chain and over it he wore a coat of black figured velvet edged with sable.

He looked more like a prince than a priest.

Around his neck in a nod to his chosen profession hung a rosary of polished garnet beads at the end of which dangled a crucifix studded with rubies, a present from the Cardinal.

Others of the Cardinal's servants might wear his livery but Henry Medwall dressed in the latest fashion discreetly but with a hint of flamboyance and aristocratic taste.

Yet he was no aristocrat.

Like Morton he came from a relatively humble background, one of the rising middle classes clambering the social ladder from the ranks of 'trade'. By his own excellence as a scholar and diplomat and his exceptional talent for staging such spectacles as was now in progress he had risen in the service of a great master.

He had two rectories, one near Calais and one at Norwich but had rarely been seen at either.

His confidential services to the Cardinal were regarded as so indispensable he was hardly seen out of the shadow of that dominant personality but it was a shadow he was happy to be in for the Cardinal's shadow was as sunshine to other men.

Although nominally he was the Cardinal's confessor the confidential services he offered were seldom of the religious kind.

According to the rolls his contribution to the household was principally 'educational'.

The records showed that he had joined the Cardinal's household in 1484 at the age of eighteen whence he had been sent from Winchester Cathedral in his native Hampshire to study music with a master.

As the War of the Roses reached its climax he had gone into exile with Morton, then Bishop of Ely and unsuccessful rebel, and lived with him in Flanders as a 'tutor'.

There had been many whispers on the back stairs about this entry in the register.

Whom did he tutor? The Cardinal as befitted a senior

clergyman was unmarried and had no children that anyone knew about.

To be sure there were the children of the household but in Flanders would they not need a tutor who could speak Flemish? Why did the Cardinal need to employ an eighteen year old tutor when he was himself an educated man in middle age?

Backstairs gossip. One should not take it too seriously. Besides, jealousy aside, the whole country acknowledged Henry Medwall's merit. He was well-liked. Not only was he a charming fellow with a talent for diplomacy he was that most dangerous and desperate of characters at a time of political uncertainty, a playwright.

At a time when one had to be careful not to offend an authoritarian and suspicious government it was pleasant to hear one's rebellious thoughts voiced on the stage even if it was only in a story.

Henry Medwall was a clever and brave fellow. Everyone was agreed on that.

A fanfare from the Watergate sent Henry Medwall rushing to the window. A barge had tied up at the landing pier.

He craned his neck to see which party was entering the palace from the riverside.

A party of twelve came into the courtyard. It was the Flemish Ambassador with his officials and six musicians.

That was at any rate a blessing for the Flemish Ambassador had promised to furnish from his own household a group, according to his boast, of the most remarkable musicians in Europe.

The band consisted of two Italians, one Frenchman, a Spaniard, a German and a young Fleming, a simpleton in many ways, the son of a boatman, but gifted beyond imagination in the playing of the viol and when he sang it was said his voice could make angels weep.

Were he not so shy by nature and bereft of strong wits his name would by now have been known to everyone in England.

His name was Peter Warbeck, known as Peterkin or Perkin for short.

Henry had never heard of him. Looking down from the window he deduced that he was the fair young man with the viol.

He reminded him of someone but for the moment he couldn't think who it was he brought to mind.

He was handsome certainly with the looks of a prince in a troubadour romance.

With those looks, if his voice was as melting and sweet as the Ambassador claimed, he would charm the ladies just as long evidently as they did not fall into conversation with him. It was the Ambassador's opinion that although his manners were as polished as any gentleman – he had spent the better part of his life in the courts of Princes and the houses of great men and something of their courtesy was bound to rub off – it would be well if he were not tempted beyond the utterance of a few formal pleasantries for anyone who tested his wits was apt to find he had not much upstairs.

Henry summoned his music master and bade him go directly to the servants' hall, round up the musicians and set them to rehearsing their parts as soon as possible.

However the musicians were only part of the company required for the performance of his new play.

Fretfully he continued to watch from the window while keeping an eye on the general preparations.

The Spanish Ambassador arrived with his retinue also rowed over from the Palace of Westminster where he was a guest of the King.

The Spaniards were overdressed as only Spaniards know how and a detachment of armed men brought up the rear.

He frowned a little at the sight of them. It was not unusual for an ambassador to be accompanied by his own bodyguard when travelling by road but such a precaution seemed unnecessary on a river crossing when he was only to attend a party.

The guards seemed to be huddled tightly around a hunched figure mysteriously hooded and shrouded in a voluminous cloak.

Henry raised his eyebrows at the sight of this mysterious interloper who seemed by some oversight to be missing from the guest list. His arrival was clearly shrouded in secrecy. It was so secret in fact that the Cardinal had not even mentioned it to his confidential secretary but he had worked for Morton long enough to know better than to be surprised at unscheduled comings and goings.

The Cardinal himself hurried into the courtyard to personally welcome his most important guest.

The Spanish Ambassador like all hidalgos stood very much upon ceremony and was extremely careful of his dignity.

The Cardinal welcomed him warmly with all due formality and ushered him into the Palace pausing briefly to lay a hand on the shoulder of the uninvited one. Clearly he knew the face under the hood.

The Spanish party filed into the Palace in search of some warmth and conviviality on that freezing day, conditions which they found more onerous than most being used to warmer climes.

Henry continued to stand with his eyes fixed on the Palace gates anxiously watching and waiting.

Nothing.

Then – at last and not before time - a covered wagon came trundling through the park from the direction of Southwark.

Henry could see it rumbling through the avenue of trees partly because the branches were bare and partly because it was painted all the colours of the rainbow.

Alongside it marched a company of Mummers in various stages of costume, some with a Spanish some with a Flemish flavour.

At the head of a pair of Shire horses pulling what was under its canvas a heavy brewer's dray marched a Roman Senator in full armour, his toga swathed around a golden breastplate that directed the sun into everybody's eyes creating a dazzling aura.

On the seat of the wagon sat an even more impressive figure.

Although of modest height he managed to give the impression that he was larger than life by the imperial manner with which he hailed those who stood by in fact and those who stood by only in his imagination who were myriads more.

He wore a scarlet hat of such exaggerated proportions that no Florentine Duke would have dared dispute the title "The Magnificent" with him seeing the way he swept it before him, now proud, now condescending.

Beside him sat two 'ladies' swathed in veils and crowned with garlands of flowers never seen at this season.

Henry recognized the crowns of Flora and Ver, Goddesses of Spring, which were part of the May-Day wardrobe but here pressed into the services of classical drama for the piece he had written was the very pretty interlude of "*Fulgens and Lucres*".

Everyone knew that the maidens were in fact boys for at that date in England no woman was allowed to set foot on a stage but notwithstanding that and the fact that the weather was not conducive to passion the accompanying crowd cheered them as enthusiastically as if they had been the rarest beauties.

Henry smiled. Now he could relax and feel confident in his plans for the festivities.

The Players had arrived.

Chapter Two

The Spanish Alliance

The Ambassadors had come to the party well before the other guests in order to have a private meeting with the King's chief minister before the festivities began.

It was the culmination of a series of talks that had been continuing over the past few weeks ever since their Excellencies were presented at the court of King Henry VII of England.

On the surface the talks were all about trade. Trade with Flanders had become particularly vital to English interests and during the previous year Cardinal Morton had successfully negotiated a trade agreement with Archduke Philip known as the *Intercursus Magnus* or Great Treaty because of its commercial importance.

However on this occasion the meat of the matter went beyond import licences and customs' duties.

The purpose of the Ambassadors' visit to London was to negotiate the betrothal of eleven year old Prince Arthur to Princess Catherine of Aragon, daughter of King Ferdinand of Spain.

Thus it was that the meeting in the privy chamber was formally convened with both Ambassadors present with their respective retinues of officials together with the secretariat of the Chancellery and sundry senior members of the Chapter of Westminster Abbey, all of whom were required to witness the signing of the betrothal documents.

The Spanish Ambassador was in particular a stickler for formalities.

Pedro de Ayala had begun his career as secretary to King

Ferdinand, then served his wife Queen Isabella and married her lady in waiting.

Cardinal Morton recalled that he was not regarded as a learned man having been educated only in those subjects considered necessary for the enlightenment of a gentleman but he had a reputation for being clever (cleverness in a political sense not necessarily going hand in hand with wisdom) and extremely discreet.

When the marriage alliance had first been mooted Cardinal Morton had taken the opportunity to link it to a treaty between England and Scotland, the Scots at that time being allies of Spain.

With pressure on Scotland's King James, if peace between England and Scotland was barely imaginable, Morton hoped at least they might negotiate a pragmatic truce.

His plans had been approved by Ferdinand and Isabella who were extremely keen to secure a suitable husband for the Princess of Aragon but almost immediately scuppered by Henry VII of England who demanded peremptorily of James of Scotland that as a condition of the treaty he must surrender the Pretender Richard of York.

King James declined to accept this condition pointing out that he was related to the young man by marriage and he deemed it would be dishonourable on his part to deliver up to certain death a man who was his kinsman.

As the Scottish King stood upon this point of honour the Spanish King and Queen saw an opportunity to ingratiate themselves further with their daughter's future father-in-law.

They dispatched Pedro de Ayala to the draughty passages of Edinburgh to soothe and un-ruffle Scottish feathers and find a solution to this *impasse.*

Finding King James implacable in the defence of a kinsman he solved the problem in a typically pragmatic Spanish way.

He simply lured the object of the controversy into his confidence and kidnapped him.

The King of Scotland might have felt that as a matter of honour he could not surrender the Yorkist prince but the King of Spain was under no such obligation.

In this way Ayala reasoned the King of Spain would contrive the surrender and the honour of the Scots would be maintained.

On this basis he had offered to deliver the prisoner into Cardinal Morton's custody under cover of the Christmas feast to prevent any riot or public demonstration.

London was a notoriously volatile city but Christmas was the most important feast for Englishmen, half heretic as they were, and they would all be too drunk for a full twelve days with their pagan 'wassail' to take any interest in this vital shift in the political landscape.

Consequently when the Ambassador entered the Privy Chamber followed by his extravagantly dressed retinue he was a man well pleased with himself and confident in his good fortune.

He had achieved his aim and secured the interests of his Sovereign from whom he could now expect marks of high favour.

He was a man who could not now be moved.

He strolled sedately to the table on which the various documents had been set out and took his seat with stately dignity.

Morton was mildly amused.

"So it is agreed your Excellency that we may proceed to sign the marriage contract?"

The Spaniard inclined his head in slight, very slight but significant acknowledgement.

"This marriage," went on the Cardinal addressing his remarks to the whole room and in his mind to posterity, "will furnish us with the great opportunity to create a lasting peace between our nations. Five years ago Cristofero Columbus discovered lands to the west which he claimed for Spain. Earlier this year Captain John Cabot sailed from Bristol and landed in the New Found Land to the North. To the best of our belief these new Territories stretch over vast distances from north to south of the Atlantic Ocean. Bound together by this alliance Spain and England can share dominion of these new lands."

There was an appreciative murmur as the splendid opportunities offered by the new discoveries and the peaceful trading conditions necessary to exploit them were considered by all present.

"Above all," sermonized the Cardinal as befitted a senior churchman, "this is an opportunity for peace. When I first came to the Holy See of Canterbury as Archbishop I preached a sermon on the text: 'Depart from evil and do good, speak peace and pursue it' and this has been my whole policy as a Minister in the Government of England. Peace is not a state of lethargy but a positive thing. The pursuit of peace is a duty to be undertaken by us all. Peace, my dear brethren, is better than war."

He did not add on this occasion, as he had on another, that one *may* wage war, not only with the apostle a spiritual war but also a corporeal war provided that the cause was just, the war publicly proclaimed and the rules of humanity observed.

If the Ambassador felt tempted to remind him of his words now he suppressed the urge and politely applauded the Christian spirit His Eminence had introduced into the occasion.

"There is however," interposed the Flemish Ambassador silkily, "the matter of the Condition."

The Cardinal sat back in his chair and thoughtfully assessed the Flemish Ambassador.

Unlike his Spanish counterpart he was not statesmanlike and dignified. He was a short, energetic man with the pugnacious features of a bulldog, not pretty but effective.

He was not a man given to diplomatic rodomontades. He was courteous but in a bluff, outspoken way. When he spoke he was direct and to the point. Morton rather liked him. He had little time for the airs and graces still less the corrupt and petty intrigues of courtiers like Don Dinero has he had privately christened the ambitious Spanish grandee.

The Flemish Ambassador was a practical, hard-headed politician. Like Morton he had a sound grasp of economics and was a man with a flexible point of view. Morton had spent many years in exile in Flanders so he knew his type and admired him.

"We have considered the Condition," acknowledged the Spaniard with another slight, very slight inclination of the head, "and His Majesty King Ferdinand has agreed to accept it."

The witnesses looked baffled as well they might, having no knowledge of this hitherto secret part of the negotiations. Cardinal Morton took pity on them.

"His Majesty King Henry has made it a condition of the betrothal that his Majesty the King of Spain, who has hitherto supported the rebellion of the Pretender who calls himself Richard IV of England, cease forthwith to countenance his claim and give succour to his enemies but instead to surrender to the King's Majesty the said rebel and pretender for the security of his realm."

"It cannot be denied," pointed out the Flemish Ambassador, "that Prince Richard has the better claim."

The Spanish Ambassador was haughtily dismissive of this suggestion although he had been arguing in favour of this point of view for the past six years. Such is the contrary nature of diplomacy.

"The matter has been examined by our most eminent scholars and men of law and His Majesty King Ferdinand has accepted their advice thus. His Majesty's support of the Prince's claim was correct insofar that he is the son of the late Edward IV of this realm and his legitimate heir notwithstanding the late King Richard's Act of Parliament declaring him illegitimate, which His Majesty King Ferdinand regards as a mere instrument of expediency and takes no cognizance of. Thus His Majesty took the view that he had the better claim in English law. However the dynastic wars of recent years between the Houses of Lancaster and York have – what is your English expression – muddied the waters."

The Ambassador smiled at his own condescension in allowing himself a little English colloquialism.

"King Henry," he went on, "is the great-great-grandson of the Duke of Gaunt who was King of Castile. King Ferdinand is both King of Aragon and Regent of the Kingdom of Castile. Therefore in the light of the betrothal of Prince Arthur to Princess Catherine His Majesty is bound to recognize his future son-in-law's possible claim to the throne of Castile. It is therefore agreed between the Sovereigns that in return for His Majesty's acknowledgement that Henry Tudor is the rightful and legitimate heir of the Crown of England which shall pass to his son Arthur hereafter King Henry will repudiate any claim he might be said to possess to the throne of Castile which he will defend as the birthright of King Ferdinand's son now nominated Philip of Castile. On this understanding His Majesty accepts the condition as laid down by King Henry and delivers today the Pretender, Richard of York, into the custody of the Archbishop of Canterbury trusting in his Grace's Christian mercy to see that the young man is housed and cared for according to his gentlemanly, indeed noble, antecedents."

There was a tiny but audible gasp that ran around the room. Poor rebel who has no Spanish Kingdom to bargain with!

The rebellion of Richard of York had rumbled on for the past six years threatening to undo all that had been achieved by Henry and Morton in healing the deep divisions between the houses of Lancaster and York.

Richard's claim had been upheld by Flanders, France, Ireland and Spain and by the King of Scotland who had approved the marriage of the handsome young Prince to his own cousin Lady Katharine Gordon and above all by his aunt Margaret the formidable Duchess of Burgundy.

This European alliance had threatened to destroy the fragile stability of the newly unified realm of England and undo all the commercial advantage that its merchants had lately seized.

To remove this threat acting in his capacity as Chancellor of the Exchequer was Morton's main aim.

However it was not a policy that met with the approval of all the European powers.

Flanders lay between Burgundy and England hence the Flemish Ambassador had been called upon by the Dowager Duchess to see fair play and secure as far as possible the safe conduct of her nephew.

Morton was walking a tricky tightrope. The Yorkist prince had powerful friends.

He held out his hands one to grasp the arm of either Ambassador and bathed each of his guests with his surprisingly warm smile for he was a man they both would have described as formidable rather than friendly.

"Then the marriage contract may be signed," he said emotionally. "Let us not lose sight of our main objective. It was on Christmas Day that King Henry signed the marriage contract to marry our beautiful Queen Elizabeth, the mother of our hopeful prince. Their match brought peace to England. Today we sign the contract for their son Arthur to marry the Princess of Aragon. This match will bring peace to Europe. Let us go forward gentlemen and, like the first Arthur, our prince's namesake, institute a Golden Age."

He passed the contract across the table and the Spanish Ambassador signed with a flourish.

The Flemish Ambassador paused for a moment as if wondering whether he should reconsider but then deciding further objection would not answer witnessed the document.

The secretaries dived forward to blot the damp ink and affixed ribbons and seals.

Rings were pressed into the warm wax and the formalities were thus concluded.

The betrothal of Prince Arthur to Princess Catherine of Aragon was now complete.

The marriage would take place in four years' time since Prince Arthur was still too young to take on the responsibilities of a husband but for now the alliance between their two countries was successfully sealed.

Chapter Three

The King's Players

The Players entered the hall with a flourishing drum-roll and a solo fanfare on a trumpet fashioned in the appearance of a large shell.

Henry Medwall laughed but his fellow servants applauded as the Florentine Duke stepped forward.

"Know we are the *lusores regis*," announced the Magnificent in the extraordinary hat displaying even more extraordinary vowels, "*alias, in lingua Anglicana, les playars* of the Kings interludes fresh from the triumphant presentation at Sheen of "The Conversion of St Paul" with four live horses, lightning and fervents, the descent of a dove and an angel from heaven on separate occasions and the ascent of devils from Hell who then vanish away in a fiery flame and tempest to the great alarm of the ladies and the consternation of the gentlemen."

The advertisement completed he bowed again so low as to sweep the floor with his enormous hat inviting the plaudits of the crowd who duly obliged.

The actor who had led the horses dressed as a Roman senator held out his hand to Henry.

"Welcome John," said Henry shaking his hand warmly for John English was the leader of the King's Players and an old friend.

"Let me introduce you to your players Master Medwall," declared John English projecting his voice so that he could be heard by the entire room as well as the man next to him. He indicated them one by one with a sweeping gesture.

"William Rastell will play Cornelius."

A burst of applause from the audience. William Rastell who took the parts of “young men about town” made an elegant leg.

“Thomas Tiptoft who will play Old Father Fulgens.”

Thomas Tiptoft was an older man, suitably grizzled in his make-up underneath which he was still vigorous and strong in late middle age. He played elderly characters fathers, saints, popes, ancient prophets and God being his speciality but he was nowhere near as old as the characters he played.

“The boys will play Lady Lucres and her maid Joan,” continued John English a trifle dismissively passing over the two ‘ladies’ who shrank back behind the others. He waved them off and sent them scurrying to the ‘tiring-room’ set aside for them off the corridor just outside the Great Hall; ‘and I will play the hero Gaius Flaminius, and this..” he paused for effect before he introduced the last member of the company, “is Miles Bloomfield, actor, who will play you a ranting Herod for sixpence, a black Iniquity for tuppence and any vice you care to mention for a penny three farthings."

"Odsbodikins!" protested Miles. "You do me too little honour Englishman. Thus little you do besmall me to my great expediency. I can play the villain! *Can* I play the villain?" *(Cheers)* "I can rant and rage and stare all about! I can pull out a poignard and put your eyes out! I can play you a villainous varlet most viley. You will tremble to see me have my wicked way! But is this all? No! My fame is spread from the orient to the occident as an oculist and alchemist. I have the potestation of potions." *(Seizing a giggling maid)* "Do you need an elixir of love to heal an unrequited ache of the heart?" *(Pointing out a laughing footman)* Or a cure for that universal disease bone-idleness or malingering? I can cast you any number of spells and incantations for a small gratuity. As witness of my extraordinary ingenuity I refer you to my late "The Conversion of St Paul" with four live horses, lightning and fervents, the descent of a dove and an angel on separate occasions and the ascent of devils from Hell who then vanished away in fiery flames and a tempest of which I have the honour to be The Author."

Miles favoured Henry with a brilliant smile, swept off his hat again and bowed with so exaggerated an air of courtesy that he nearly overbalanced onto his nose.

"My suavious solace and singular recreatory, my predelict special," he cooed in tones so dulcet they might have been addressed to a woman, "I bid you *osculare fundamentum*!"

Henry Medwall looked at John English with a raised eyebrow.

"Do I hear correctly or did he just ask me to kiss his backside?"

There was a general collapse around the hall as the maids fell into unseemly giggles and the menservants were convulsed in laughter.

Master Miles looked pained. "*Damnant ingratum,*" he complained. "Damn your ingratitude! Did I not offer you my affectionate respects from the very bottom of my heart? It's all a matter of translation. Latin is so very ambiguous."

"There never was among Christians less charity than there is among playwrights," observed Henry Medwall accurately. "It appeared to me you were offering me something quite other."

Master Miles drew himself up to nearly average height and replaced his hat to add a few more inches.

"I discommend and disallow this often mutability!" he retorted consciously quoting his own lines. "To every creature thou art dispectuous and odible."

"Odible?"

"Odible."

"Miles, there is no such word as odible."

Miles was offended.

"Your criminous complaint woundeth my heart as a lance," he

sniffed. "I am an alchemist with words as well as master of the elements. In the crucible of my fancy I take the rough-hewn rocks of the *lingua Anglicana* and transmute them with the philosopher's stone that is the poetic art. I say you are odible and odible you are."

"If it please your negligence," conceded Henry magnanimously, "I beg your pardon. *Nec in hasa, nec in gladio, salvat Dominus.* Neither in the spear nor the sword does our Lord rejoice."

He bowed as low as Miles had done and executed a near pratfall with as much skill and grace just saving himself from overbalancing at the last moment.

"A great doctor of benign complexion and the true preacher of the high divinity, a very pinnacle of the faith!" declared Master Bloomfield with all the fervour of an actor who knows he has a well-paid engagement.

This assessment of Master Medwall's character being generally approved cordial relations were restored.

"Miles, Tom and William go and bring in the props," ordered John English getting down to business for such matters were not to be trusted to servants as the prop-baskets contained secrets of the dramatic arts the players wished to keep to themselves. "Henry, come with me. I have two new boys both excellent in the portrayal of the fair sex. A man might almost lose is heart to them if he were not aware of their masculine gender."

He said this loudly again so everyone in the room could hear.

Henry was a trifle put out. It would be the first performance of his play and the highlight of the year's entertainment. It was hardly the time to try out new performers.

"As long as they know their lines," he grumbled.

John English noted his expression and was all balm and self-confidence.

"Word perfect," he assured him. "Perfect in every way and young Jonathan you know is suffering with his voice breaking. He cannot speak a line without shifting from treble to bass and it is disconcerting to have the heroine begin with a soft small voice and then descend to a bass baritone."

Henry allowed that this was a disadvantage of using boy actors that could not be helped.

"And Harry?"

"Measles. Face all blotchy. Not an inch of greasepaint could make him pass for a pretty maid today."

Henry sighed but he was accustomed to the vagaries of the stage.

"Very well. These two new boys are well enough rehearsed?"

"Rehearsed them myself. They will astound you. Come and see for yourself."

He led Henry out of the hall and along a corridor to two side chambers that had been reserved as dressing rooms for the actors.

John English had been most specific that they must have two rooms although Henry could not think why.

Through the door of the first room he could see Miles and Tom struggling with a large hamper containing props and costumes for the Mummers.

The door to the second room was closed.

John knocked politely and waited until he was bidden to enter.

Inside they found the two heroines of the play still draped in thick veils.

John closed the door behind him and took the precaution of locking it then motioned to the ladies to lift their veils.

Henry's expression changed from mild curiosity to utter astonishment as he looked from one 'boy' to the other.

Even allowing for the wonders of theatrical make-up he had never seen boy actors look more beautiful than the two ladies he saw before him now.

One of them was a slender beauty of a little more than twenty years with red hair, a freckled skin and pale complexion that suggested a Hibernian Celt.

Her eyes were large and green like a cat's.

The other lady, a few years older, with hair as a summer cornfield and eyes as blue as the Mediterranean, was at least her peer in beauty despite the fact that she was the mother of two hopeful sons and above her in honour for Henry recognized her immediately.

He dropped to one knee and kissed her hand.

"Your Majesty!"

Chapter Four

The Queen's Pleasure

Queen Elizabeth's smile dimpled her cheeks and her eyes danced.

"You must not kneel to me Master Medwall. You must know I am in disguise. You are the Master here."

Henry Medwall for once was lost for words.

"How is it, you are wondering, that I have joined the King's Players?" his lady prompted him.

He nodded still speechless.

She turned to her companion and introduced her.

"This is Princess Katharine that is cousin to the King of Scotland and my sister-in-law."

Henry took a moment to work this out.

"She is the Princess of York, Prince Richard's Scots wife."

The Queen nodded. Then overcome with emotion she grasped his hand.

"Oh my dear friend Henry, you have always taken care of my brothers through all their years of exile. You were there when Edward died and held his hand when I could not. I beg you do not desert us now."

"Madam," he assured her, "my life is yours. How can I do you service?"

"You know that this feast is in honour of the two ambassadors?"

Henry nodded. Naturally as the confidential secretary of Cardinal Morton he was aware of the importance of the event.

"Do you know of the other secret matter that is to be decided here tonight apart from the betrothal of my son Arthur to the Spanish Infanta?"

Henry considered before replying whether he should know of this or not and decided his best course was to remain enigmatically silent.

Queen Elizabeth again prompted him.

"Do you know of the Condition?"

Here she had him stumped. What condition could she be referring to? He did not think she could mean the condition of the Spanish Infanta since she and Prince Henry had not yet met and they were both still children.

Seeing she had drawn a blank she sighed and Lady Katharine took up the tale.

"My husband is the price of this marriage contract. He is to be surrendered and imprisoned this very hour."

"But how Majesty..? The King of Scotland refused to give him up."

"We believed we were safe in Scotland but he was tricked into going to meet the Spanish Ambassador on Arthur's Seat. He had no reason not to go. The Spanish were our allies or so we believed. When he arrived at the appointed place he was seized by men of the Ambassador's bodyguard and bundled away to a ship bound for Spain. It was all the Ambassador's doing. We have been betrayed."

Arthur's seat! That is the name of the rocky outcrop that overshadows the city of Edinburgh. The Spanish Ambassador was not a man inclined to wit but he did a nice line in dry irony.

Tears welled in the eyes of the pretty princess and trickled down her cheeks. Henry was a priest but he was also a man. He was not immune.

His mind went back to the muffled prisoner he had seen being brought up from the Watergate and the way in which the Cardinal had affectionately touched him on the shoulder.

Of course the prisoner was the Prince and the gesture was meant to reassure him.

But how reassure him? If his surrender was the price of the marriage alliance there was surely not much the Cardinal could do.

He must be lodged somewhere in the Palace under lock and key.

"You must help us Henry," begged the Queen. "Katharine and I cannot let Richard be confined in the Tower again from which he will never escape. I cannot allow my husband to execute my own brother. You understand my predicament. For my son I am glad of this alliance but for my brother I am filled with horror. Katharine has a ship, a swift caravel, waiting at Greenwich. It will sail on the midnight tide. My brother must be on that ship. Help us Henry. We beg you. You are our only hope."

Master Medwall was for the moment nonplussed.

"If it is your Majesty's pleasure.." he stammered. "But how

are you come to be with the King's Players?"

John English looked slightly apologetic.

"It seemed the safest way to get the ladies into the palace," he excused himself. "And they are word perfect I assure you. No-one will suspect that the boys playing the ladies are in fact ladies although they will be astounded at their verisimilitude."

Henry was barely listening. His quick mind had already moved on to consider the workings of the plot.

The prince would remain in the palace only for the duration of the feast.

Once it was concluded he would be rowed up the river to the Tower of London and the chance to rescue him would be lost perhaps forever.

Fortunately the Thames is a tidal river and the passage under London Bridge was notoriously difficult against the tide. The tide would not turn seaward again until the stroke of midnight at which time the watermen would begin rowing the prisoner downriver to the Tower.

At that same time they must be in Greenwich with the prince aboard the caravel ready to put to sea.

The clock began to strike the hour. Five o'clock. It was already dark and soon the guests for the banquet would be arriving. Just seven hours. But then he was a genius. Wasn't he?

Chapter Five

Plots and Stratagems

In the Cardinal's Cabinet, a small room set aside for private study and well-panelled for confidentiality, John Morton sat in consultation with the Flemish Ambassador.

No secretaries were present to record their conversation. This discussion was to be entirely between the two of them.

Both men acknowledged to each other that the situation was awkward.

"The position of Flanders is ambiguous," explained the Flemish Ambassador. "Archduke Philip is anxious to maintain good trading relations with England. Our weavers need your English wool. On the other hand the Burgundians are our nearest neighbours and to fall foul of the temper of the Dowager Duchess Margaret by failing to come to the aid of her nephew is not in our best interests."

"This alliance will secure peace between England and Spain and permit our ships to trade unmolested with the new territories. Spain will keep to the south and England to the north of the Americas. This is agreed. The improved wealth and security of England can only benefit Flanders since it is in the interests of the English to protect your weavers on either side of the Channel."

"Naturally you wish the alliance to proceed," acknowledged the Flemish Ambassador. "Archduke Philip has no objection in principle but as for the person of the Prince he wonders if there might not be some room for accommodation. He has been your protégé for many years. You do not intend that he should lose his head?"

Cardinal Morton raised his hands and spread them wide in a gesture to signify his helplessness in the matter.

“He has been like a son to me,” he admitted sadly. “I am very fond of him. If it were left to me…” his voice tailed off but then he resumed in a business-like tone, “but my sovereign has laid down this onerous condition and it is my duty to secure the alliance. If I could see a way in which the prince could be saved…but I can see no way that would not damage all that has been achieved. Ordinarily I would trust in King Henry’s mercy. He is not a vindictive man but in this case all depends upon his own sovereignty remaining unchallenged and unchecked. It has been my life’s training to put the affairs of God and State before my own interests. I love the Prince. I love my Sovereign Lord. How are these two conflicting interests to be reconciled? One must trust in God and have faith that whatever his dispositions they are for the best.”

The Flemish Ambassador leaned forward a little closer to ensure that his words could not be heard by someone, say, listening at the keyhole.

"One may trust in God but sometimes it is better not to wait for him to take action. If the matter could be concluded without the sacrifice of the Prince," urged the Flemish Ambassador, "you would not be sorry if such a thing could be arranged? Nor would King Henry I'll wager since the Prince is his wife's brother and she, as I have been informed, is very fond of him. The peace of the King's marriage may be at stake here. Concord in matrimony is a very desirable state I'm sure you'll agree."

The Cardinal nodded. "Matrimony is a holy state. We must do all we can to preserve it."

The Flemish Ambassador leaned in a little closer still and his voice dropped to barely a whisper.

"I may be frank here? It is the wish of the Dowager Duchess and the

Archduke Philip that this matter may be brought off in such a way as to satisfy all parties. My orders – I see no point in beating about the bush – are to rescue the Prince if it is at all possible to do so without the destruction of the alliance."

"And how may this be done?" inquired the Cardinal. "The Prince is in my cellar under lock and key and an armed detachment of Spanish guards. If he were to simply disappear I fear I might be deemed guilty in some measure of negligence if not treason. Tonight he will be transferred to the Tower where escape will be impossible. The marriage contract has been signed and the prisoner delivered. The Condition has been met. There is no going back now."

The Flemish Ambassador's face lit up with a little secret smile.

"Obviously any escape must be brought off in such a way as to ensure your Excellency is above suspicion. It will be difficult," he admitted but then added with a gleam in his eye, "but not impossible."

Cardinal Morton looked him in the eye and then, with something of a gleam in his own, he summoned an attendant and bade him "Send for Master Medwall."

Chapter Six

The Princes in the Tower

It was the 23rd April 1484 and the morning of St George's Day.

The choir of St Paul's cathedral had been summoned to the Tower to sing for the Royal Household in the chapel an anthem composed in honour of England's relatively new patron saint.

Walking slowly and solemnly at the rear of the procession behind the double row of small boy sopranos and trebles, slowly and solemnly because the little ones in front could not walk very fast without breaking into an impious run, came the older choristers who provided the tenor and bass.

Among them was Henry Medwall eighteen years old. He was a fair tenor but the breaking of his voice in adolescence had not transmuted the heavenly purity of his soprano to his adult voice. He could not see a life in music ahead of him and had already become bored with life in the choir stalls where he was conscious he did not and could not shine.

He had begun like most young men to look for a life of adventure and this was the very first day of that new life.

Or possibly, if he were not to be successful, the very last.

St George's Day was marked in the City of London by the usual trade fair, this time spread out along the wharfs and steps in front of the Hanseatic warehouses and the Customs House.

Consequently the procession of choristers made slow progress as they made their way along the riverside from St Paul's.

Henry Medwall did not mind. It gave him time to think.

He had been singled out by the Bishop of Ely as a young man of particular promise.

John Morton had been impressed by the swift way in which he had grasped the subtleties of the situation.

Which were as follows.

A year earlier King Richard, now the third of that title, had been the Lord Protector of the Council and ruled as Regent for his young nephew Edward V but the instability of the country still teetering on the brink of civil war made it unwise to have a boy-king on the throne.

Edward had been quietly set aside quite legally by Act of Parliament which declared him and his brother Richard illegitimate by reason of the doubtful legality of Edward IV's marriage to their mother Elizabeth Woodville. This was something of a fiction but Parliament approved the Act as a peaceful means of contriving the transfer of power from nephew to uncle.

The young princes were sent to live in the Tower, the most fortified of all London's Royal Palaces not least because it housed the Royal Mint, in case King Richard's enemies (and he had many) attempted to seize the boys and use them as ammunition against him.

In spite of this their Woodville relatives, their mother's pushy and ambitious family, continued to foment rebellion urging that Edward had been deposed unfairly because his parents' marriage had been valid.

This in addition to the Lancastrian claim which continued to shake the foundations of the state meant the lives of the young princes were in constant danger.

The Tower was the safest place for them to be. Although a strong fortress it was still also in constant use as a royal palace and within the sturdy walls it was like a small village its towers dotted around a pretty green alongside which stood the Chapel of St George.

Here the boys lived quite comfortably in their own quarters with their own servants and took part in all the activities of the community made up of the Royal family, noble guests, the Palace staff and men-at-arms.

On St George's Day like everyone else they put on their finest clothes and set out across Tower Green to the Chapel of St George to celebrate the saint's day in the church consecrated to his name.

At the same time Henry Medwall walking slowly towards them in the rear of the choir was considering how he could safely bring the boys out of the Tower.

Chapter Seven

The Wicked Uncle

A week earlier Henry Medwall had been summoned to accompany John Morton, then Bishop of Ely, to the palace at Richmond known as Sheen where he was to meet the King.

Henry had heard much of King Richard III. He was a hunchback they said. Ugly like a toad.

When they were shown into the King's Cabinet the first thing he noticed was that the King did indeed have a hunch. It was his left shoulder that was severely misshapen although when he was sitting up straight you could not see it.

Henry noticed that he did not make any attempt to disguise his deformity. He wore a plain quilted tunic which did not hide it although as a token to other people's sensibilities perhaps the King drew attention from it by slinging a scarf and a large hat over his shoulder so that he so to speak wore his hat on his hump which made it less noticeable.

Otherwise there was not much of the monarch about him. He was by no means ugly, indeed about his face and features he was a personable even good-looking man dark and saturnine unlike his fair-haired brothers and sisters but in no way toad-like or unfriendly. His smile on welcoming them into the room was wan but charming.

He looked sad and tired Henry thought. He was a man in mourning. He had just lost his frail son soon after the death of his wife Anne and buried him in Yorkshire.

The long journey back to London walled in by grief had given him time to consider the further complications this death presented the state.

He greeted the Bishop courteously and with an affection that slightly surprised his young companion since John Morton was notorious for his support for the Lancastrian cause.

He had been among those who rebelled when Richard seized the Crown.

Only six months earlier he had joined the rebellion of the Duke of Buckingham but seeing there was no support for the enterprise he had abandoned the plot and fled into exile in Flanders.

But in politics unlikely friendships can grow up among politicians washed by the ebb and flow of political realities.

Richard, whatever his faults, was a man who recognized ability and he recognized his own need for the advice of a wily and impartial judge.

Bishop Morton was a skilful political operator and his only

interest was in securing the peace and security of the people of England.

Accordingly only a month after he had escaped to Flanders the King invited him back with the offer of a pardon.

There were those who suspected he may already have been won to the King's cause when he left the side of the Duke of Buckingham, but Buckingham's supporters regarded him merely as man who always backed the winning side.

Certainly from the Lancastrian point of view his loyalty was beyond question because in December when Richard made it a condition of a treaty with France that Henry Tudor then seeking refuge in Brittany should be surrendered to his enemies Morton sent him word from Flanders giving him time to evade capture and so Henry always believed saved his life.

In spite of this apparent sympathy for the Lancastrian cause Richard continued to woo Morton's support.

In January he convened the first Parliament for many years and in almost its first Act Bishop Morton was forgiven the death penalty on the grounds that he was a clergyman although his "temporalities" (his secular estates) were confiscated.

So it was that the way was cleared for him to return to England and that was the reason that at the beginning of April he was at the King's side ready to offer him advice on the succession.

Henry was subdued by the oppressive air of sadness that hung over the Palace and in any case one did not speak to a King unless spoken to.

Richard was friendly enough. As Bishop Morton introduced Henry as one who might be helpful to him the King held out his hand and Henry bent his head and kissed the ring which carried the King's seal, a sign of his authority.

"Quite the courtier," murmured the King who appeared mildly

amused, "but I meant for you to shake it. We are quite out of Court here Master Medwall. You may be comfortable."

He indicated for them both to take a seat and sat down opposite them. A flagon stood on the table beside him and he poured each of them a glass of wine. This domestic act was so out of character both of what Henry expected in a King and all he had heard of his monarch that he was for the moment silenced.

"The death of Princes Master Medwall," said the King with a sigh, "is not merely a matter for personal grief. It creates subtle shifts in policy, in the balance of power. I have lost my son. This creates difficulty for me. It means I have no heir."

It was Morton who responded seeing Henry was lost for words. When you are eighteen it is very difficult to know how to answer death.

"Your Majesty is yet young. You may have another son."

Richard smiled.

"Would that be possible I should ask for no better son that the one I have lost. He was my heart's ease. But even if it were to be so no son of mine would be fit to rule for many years and kingship is a cherry time in these turbulent days. It would heal many differences if I could name Edward to stand next in line for the succession since he was King before me but alas I have had him declared illegitimate to give countenance to my own claim and I cannot go back on my word. You begin to see how my troubles beset me?"

Henry knew this was his opportunity to demonstrate his grasp of great affairs. He pulled himself together determined not to be over-awed by the exalted company he was keeping.

"Your Majesty cannot keep the boy too close or he becomes a focus for disaffected rebels but you may not dispose of him even," he amended recollecting that the Plantagenets were a noisy but affectionate clan, "were you, as his uncle and kinsman, prepared to commit such an abhorrent deed."

The King smiled thinly. Perhaps he was thinking of his brother George, Duke of Clarence, drowned in a butt of malmsey wine they said on the orders of his elder brother Edward.

"I have seen the untimely end of a good many friends and relatives," he said dryly, "but I have not yet sunk to making war on children. I see Master Medwall you are a young man of great perception. My lord Bishop has chosen you well."

John Morton had given Henry his chance and he had not failed him. Now he took over direction of the matter.

"If your Majesty means to stand on the illegitimacy of the King and his brother then you must look elsewhere among your nephews for your present successor."

Richard nodded.

"I had thought to name the Earl of Warwick as strictly next in line. I thought this might appease malcontents in my own party but he is a boy like the other two and even younger. This is no time for the country to be governed by a minority. If I were to die suddenly and I do not frankly look forward to passing quietly in my bed of old age then my heir must be a man schooled in the arts of war and who has some measure of the world. For this reason I have decided to name my sister's son John of Lincoln."

Morton approved the choice. John of Lincoln was eighteen years old and had already reached a man's estate.

"But there remains," Richard went on, "as Master Medwall has so shrewdly deduced, the problem of what to do with my brother's sons. Warwick is no great threat for the present while his cousins live and thrive. He is too young to be troublesome barely out of his baby clothes and in no immediate danger himself. But if I name John my heir what price for the lives of Edward and

Richard? If their legitimacy is established John's claim will fall and all that will reign when I am gone will be war and chaos all over again."

"You see Henry," his mentor told him, "the absolute necessity of removing the princes from London and from England. We must keep them safe but out of harm's way. The future is for God to decide, not Man."

"Nor Kings," amended their royal master. "I see the boy grasps the situation well enough. Well Henry, your King begs a favour of you. Will you help us in this matter?"

Henry was flattered but flustered. How could he refuse? And if he did the proper thing and dutifully offered his service what could he actually do?

Bishop Morton forestalled this obvious question.

"On St George's Day the choir of St Paul's will be summoned to sing an anthem for the Royal Household at the Tower. The two princes will be present in the chapel. They will be left alone in their pew to follow their devotions. You Henry will be three feet away in the choir stall. Now then, during the sermon you will extract them from their pew on some excuse, a call of nature will do…"

Chapter Eight

The Princes disappear

So it was that as the sermon droned on and the congregation for the most part closed their eyes and relied on the goodwill generated by their lusty singing to ease their path through Purgatory Henry slipped out of his seat at the end of the choir stall and sidled along the aisle toward the pew where the Princes sat for the moment unattended and left to endure the preacher's monotone in idleness.

They must have been primed by their uncle because they responded promptly to his casual wave towards the vestry door without question and crouching low to avoid being seen both boys scuttled into the narrow gap between the back of the choir and the outer wall where they were almost immediately hidden by Henry following behind.

As he glanced back to see if anyone had noticed him he was mildly amused by the sight of gentlemen and yeomen warders gently dozing in their pews emitting the occasional rumbling snore and the ladies sitting at the back having a quiet gossip behind their hands.

At all events no-one had noticed the Princes leave the congregation.

He followed them into the vestry where he dressed them in the robes and surplices that identified them as members of the choir.

As the service drew to a close the choir lined up to pass in procession back down the aisle while the congregation kept their eyes firmly to the front. No-one noticed the two extra choristers in front of Henry who was bringing up the rear.

They passed across Tower Green to the gate on Tower Hill where the warders stood aside to let them pass. They had no reason to challenge the choir of St Paul's.

Proceeding in a stately fashion down to the riverside they passed along the quays in front of the Italian warehouses. Here the line became undisciplined and ragged as it invariably did after a long performance as the boys began to dodge about in and out of the bales and barrels to let off steam, pushing through the crowd to view the merchandise on the stalls and making it impossible for their masters to keep a count of heads.

This Henry was relying on. After all who apart from the choirmaster counts the choir?

When they reached London Bridge Henry grasped his two charges by the collar and whisked them onto the Bridge where they were quickly lost in the throng for the shops and stalls lining the Bridge on this Fair day were overwhelmed with customers.

As they hurried across the bridge he pulled the choristers' robes off them and discarded them in a pile of second hand clothing that was for sale burying them under a pile of worn doublets under pretence of examining them.

He swept the boys along in front of him to the other side of the bridge and down the stairs where a boat had been left tied up beside a waterman's skiff. The Bishop of Ely paid a great attention to detail.

They jumped in and he set off rowing as steadily as his nerves would allow to Wapping Stairs where a ship was loading the personal effects of the Bishop who according to report had after many days of prayer and reflection declined the King's offer of a position in the government having considered the present dispute between him and the Earl of Richmond too close to call.

Leaning on the excuse that the responsibilities of his office placed upon him the obligation to remain impartial in temporal matters he was resolved to hold himself aloof and keep his distance until in the words of the chronicler 'he had experience of the sequel.'

In other words he was hedging his bets.

Those less refined in their political judgment simply jeered that Morton had yet again deftly played one side against the other and was simply looking after his own skin.

Since he had been granted a free pardon by Parliament the King was powerless to prevent him taking his leave and the wind towards Flanders was already catching at his sails.

Henry manoeuvred the rowing boat across the stream so that it came bobbing up against the side of the caravel. If there was any hue and cry on the quayside he reasoned they would be screened from it by the body of the ship.

The two princes were likely lads and skipped up the rope ladder left dangling over the side like powder monkeys.

As soon as they were all three on board they were taken below decks and kept out of sight until at last the tide turned, the sailors hauled up the gangplanks, the caravel slipped her moorings and began to move away into the centre of the stream and head steadily downriver past ever-widening banks to the estuary and at last the open sea.

Henry had burned his bridges. From now on he was Morton's man.

It had been agreed that once the boys were missed the King would hush up their disappearance.

At first it was put about that he had sent for them to go to Richmond, then to York, then to Essex to their mother and servants were sent scurrying in all directions only to return to report there was no sign of them.

It was then remembered that the King's confidential servant Sir

James Tyrrell had been seen at the Tower the night before they were missed.

Dark rumours began to circulate. When were they last seen? Were they in chapel? Someone thought they were but then someone recalled glancing in their pew at the end of the service and they were not there.

No-one associated either fact with the departure of the choir of St Paul's. A choir is such a normal part of a church service. Who would even recall that they were there?

The King was silent on the subject. The trail had gone cold. All that anyone could say for certain was that the Princes had last been seen at the Tower during the winter, when mostly they were seen indoors, and no-one had seen them since.

Meanwhile a fair wind saw them over the water and fast horses took them to the Bishop's estate in Flanders where they took up residence.

Henry became their tutor, and so he is recorded in the rolls of the Bishop's household.

By the time in 1490 Henry returned to England the youngest of the princes had reached the age of eighteen and no longer needed the services of a tutor. John Morton had already proved a successful Chancellor and been awarded the red hat of a Cardinal. Henry returned to England and after being ordained took up his position as the Cardinal's personal chaplain.

With a powerful protector Henry had nothing to fear by his association with the Yorkist princes. If King Henry had any knowledge of his part in their escape he made no mention of it. He welcomed Henry cordially to his Court as a notable scholar and talented playwright.

It appeared Henry had chosen his patron wisely.

In all the years of the rebellion he had obeyed the Cardinal's dictum that the service of the state must come before all personal considerations but in spite of that when he heard of the dashing exploits of the young prince he could not forget that he still held in affection the young boy who had, without a second thought, trusted him with his life.

Chapter Nine

In Cabinet

It was with these recollections in mind that Henry made his promise to the two anxious ladies who had cast him in the role of hero that he would rescue the Prince and see him safely out of England or perish in the attempt.

The last bit was bravado. He had no intention of perishing if he could help it.

However his first duty was to his master and he knew him well enough to know that he too must be considering how he could rescue the Prince for once he was in the Tower he could by no means be certain that the matter could be left to the King's mercy. Henry Tudor might not be personally disposed to execute his wife's brother but King Henry might have very little choice.

When he knocked at the door of the Cabinet and heard John Morton bid him enter he had not expected to find him in conference with the Flemish Ambassador.

"Come in Henry," beckoned the Cardinal. "We have need of your ingenuity."

Henry entered obediently and stood awaiting instructions.

"Did you see the party of the Spanish Ambassador arrive?" John Morton opened.

Henry nodded.

"Then you saw the prisoner."

Henry nodded again.

"Do you know who that prisoner is?"

Henry paused before nodding a third time.

"I do."

He did not offer an explanation as to how he knew and John Morton was wise enough not to ask. His confidential secretary had a habit of knowing things often before he did.

"Then you understand there is some discomfort in this situation."

Henry agreed.

"I know your Eminence holds the young man in great affection. His situation must be painful to you."

"It is and it is equally awkward for my friend the Ambassador. The nub of the situation is this. The surrender of the prisoner must take place or the alliance we have just concluded will be void but my friend the Ambassador has just put it to me that it might be possible to meet the terms of the alliance and surrender the prisoner without endangering the life and security of one we all hold in affection and esteem."

"Such a conclusion is devoutly to be wished but how is it to be achieved?"

The Flemish Ambassador's features rearranged themselves into a wolfish grin. Like most politicians he enjoyed playing games of subterfuge.

It was chess with life-size pieces on a very irregular board.

"A prisoner must be delivered to the Tower tonight that much is clear or there will be a great hue and cry which could bring us all to destruction but what if the prisoner who is delivered up to the Tower Warden is not the one we have presently in custody."

Henry's quick mind discarded some of the wilder schemes it had been toying with. This was much more practical.

"A substitution?"

He considered the plot, saw the possibility of several sub-plots and drew a conclusion satisfying to all parties.

"It could be done. The main difficulty," he mused half to himself, "would be in choosing a substitute who would not be immediately recognized as an imposter. We need to keep his identity a secret at least until half-past midnight."

"Half-past midnight?" the Cardinal echoed shrewdly spotting

that Henry had already given a rescue attempt some careful thought.

"Or thereabouts," added Henry airily. "The watermen will not leave Lambeth until midnight on account of the tide. We want to make sure the deception is not discovered until after the prisoner has disembarked at the Tower. We don't want to make it too obvious the switch was made in your cellar."

With this the Cardinal devoutly concurred.

"Also," Henry went on, "the prisoner is of a strikingly handsome person. Were he more.. ordinary it might be easier to find someone who resembled him."

"The Ambassador has already made provision for such an eventuality," Cardinal Morton pointed out inviting his companion to take the floor.

"I am instructed by the Archduke to concur with the alliance but if at all possible, to rescue the Prince if it can be contrived in such a way as will not endanger the marriage contract. I have thought long and hard about this and came to the conclusion you have just reached that is to somehow release the Prince from confinement and replace him with a substitute. For this purpose I have brought with me my musicians. You have no doubt seen them."

"I have heard them. They are practising in the gallery. Very fine."

"Well when you see them you will take note of the young man who plays the viol. His name is Peter Warbeck. He is strikingly handsome, fair, extremely like the prince provided you do not examine him too closely."

"I thought he reminded me of someone," exclaimed Henry. "I saw him coming in and it crossed my mind then that I had seen him before. Yes, by night, by candlelight, hooded and muffled as he is bound to be at this season, he should pass. Yes I see every possibility that this scheme could be made to work."

John Morton laughed. “I told you our Henry was the man for plots,” he told the Ambassador.

“So,” said the Flemish Ambassador, “the only question remains how to make the switch.”

Henry became aware that the eyes of both senior statesmen were on him. He had to do some quick thinking.

He ran over the plot again in his mind and found it foolproof.

“My play,” he pointed out, “is in two parts. Part One will be performed before the banquet then the Players leave the hall so that the guests can get on with their dinner. This will be our opportunity when everyone else is at the table and in their cups. In Part Two the Players return with the musicians, now come down from the gallery, and the Mummers. My suggestion is this. When the Players leave the hall we will proceed to the cellar and release the Prince – I assume your Eminence can furnish us with a duplicate key?”

The Cardinal nodded.

"We will substitute the Prince for the musician. Among the King's Players is an alchemist who can no doubt furnish me with a sleeping draught that will quickly overpower the young man. If he appears drunk the guards will not be able to question him. Speechless and legless he will be beyond suspicion and we believe that his appearance will pass muster in night conditions. Since the musicians will then be mingled with the players in the hall it will not be too noticeable that he is missing."

The elder statesman nodded in agreement.

"Our next problem," went on Henry warming to his work, "will be to smuggle the Prince out of the palace. This will not be difficult. We will disguise him as one of the Mummers. We have chosen, in honour of our guests to dress our Mummers in Spanish and Flemish costumes. A Spaniard may be a Moor and a Moor must naturally appear in black face. Blacked up, with a full beard and bushy eyebrows, with a turban to cover his fair hair and robes to disguise his comely shape – perhaps a false stomach – no-one will recognize him among the others. Candlelight and firelight cast interesting shadows. They are the playwright's friend."

"And the conspirator's. This is simple enough to succeed," said Morton. "The great danger is when a plot gets over-complicated. Then it is most likely to be seen through."

"We will all leave the palace together," Henry pointed out. "Mummers, Players and all. The Prince can be concealed in the wagon along with.. along with certain other parties. We will drive to The George at Southwark where he may find a swift horse and ride to Greenwich. At Greenwich he will find a ship bound for Scotland."

Cardinal Morton raised his eyebrows. He had not thought that far ahead and wondered how his confidential secretary had so far arranged things as to have even ordered the shipping arrangements.

"Scotland?"

"The King of Scotland is his wife's cousin," Henry pointed out, "and any hue and cry that the King puts in hand will naturally be directed towards the Channel ports. The ship will sail on the midnight tide and His Royal Highness will be at sea even as the substitute prisoner is being rowed downriver to the Tower. At the earliest the deception can be discovered he will be already out of the King's reach."

Cardinal Morton approved the plan.

"But what of the poor young musician," he wondered. "I would not have any harm come to him as he is an unwilling accomplice."

"No harm will come to him," the Ambassador assured him, "aside from a thick head and we Flemings are used to that. I have chosen him carefully. He is near simple-minded and although his manners are courtly and his English is good his lack of learning will betray him. I dare say he can recite you a list of the Princes of Europe having played for most of them but he has little Latin except Church Latin and while his guards may be fooled the King will only have to question him for a few minutes to know he is not the Prince. Quite apart from which, if the matter is stripped to the bone so to speak, he has one way in which he can prove he is not Richard Plantagenet."

"What is that?" inquired Henry curiously.

"He is a Jew." The Ambassador laughed coarsely. "I dare swear a Christian prince will still have his foreskin."

"If he is proved an imposter it will be well sooner rather than later. " Cardinal comforted himself. "We may be sure that our King will deal with him kindly for he did so with Lambert Simnel. When he was able to prove he was not the Earl of Warwick he simply put him to work in the kitchens. He judged he had been the instrument of other men."

"And so he will with our Peterkin be sure of it. What use

would it be to him to have him a cold corpse and were it not to be the case I should make representations to be sure since he is a citizen of my country. Your King will not want to find himself on the wrong side of Duchess Margaret. Furthermore he has been well served by the rumour that his predecessor murdered his two nephews. If he executes Richard of York he must refute this allegation for the boy cannot die twice. Then sympathy might swing back to the late King and the Yorkist rebellion take new heart. Better for him to find his prisoner is not who everyone says he is and let the whole thing live and die a hoax."

This was so sensible a viewpoint that his listeners concurred with it whole-heartedly.

The silver-tongued Cardinal felt confident that he could persuade King Henry that this outcome would be best for all parties including his own marital harmony. He therefore procured the duplicate key for Henry to conceal about his person and without further ado the plot was set in motion.

Chapter Ten

Enter the One-Eyed Knight

In the kitchens below the main hall a second performance was reaching the stage of its dress rehearsal.

The boar's head, the centrepiece of any Christmas feast in a nobleman's household, had been singed and roasted and was now being prepared for the table.

With elaborate mimicry caramelized sugar was applied to replace the hair and bristles that had been burned away.

The huge tusks had been carefully preserved and were now replaced along with eyes of coloured sugar which glowed like rubies giving the head a fearsomely life-like appearance.

An apple was polished until it shone like glass and placed in its mouth whereupon the whole was arranged on a huge silver charger and set aside on a warming stove until a fanfare would herald its arrival in the hall in great ceremony to signify that Christmas dinner could now begin.

Alongside the cooks the confectioners were busy with tarts and puddings and syllabubs putting the finishing touches to miracles of their art to grace the tables all edible but looking much too good to eat.

There were cathedrals of sugar in honour of the Cardinal and his senior churchmen, castles complete with moats and jousting knights to compliment the nobility and in recognition of their host's temporal as well as spiritual power, angels with crystal wings in honour of the occasion and nearly as faithfully recreated as that fashioned in silver gilt for the salt replicas of the

Matthew whose astonishing discoveries had been the highlight of the year, representing the importance of trade and exploration that was the reason for the presence of the ambassadors.

In the courtyard pages were being lined up and furnished with pewter flagons ready to serve mulled wine to the guests as they arrived cold from the river crossing or riding in from the park.

The players were applying powder and paint and running through their lines with the usual tumultuous jumble of mounting nerves for the guests were beginning to trickle in and within the hour they would be on.

The guests were conducted into a large antechamber where a fire roared in the grate and hot punch was being served from magnificent bowls of chased silver.

The aroma of Christmas spices hung in the air, cinnamon, nutmeg, cloves all mixed with the fruity scent of good claret, oranges and evergreen.

It is such a potent mix it immediately put a smile on the faces of the chilled visitors as they came in from the cold.

The choir of Westminster Abbey sang carols for the edification and entertainment of those present and to cover that uncomfortable hiatus when guests initially arrive and find that they do not know anybody but since the political world is a small one and politicians are not shy within a short space of time they could hardly be heard for the hubbub of conversation.

Velvet, damask, silks, satins all swirled among the more sombre black of the clerics but even they were bedecked with fur and jewels to add to the festivity of the occasion.

Eyes were meeting lighting up with the joy of recognition or not as the case may be but all was geniality. Enemies pretended to be friends for this was the season of peace as well as goodwill as Father Christmas moved among them clad in his traditional green robes a holly wreath bound round his head, dispensing jollity and generous measures of mead for those who preferred it to wine from a gigantic pewter jug.

Among the eyes that met were one – one only because its owner had lost the other and wore a leather patch to cover his disfigurement - and a pair of sparkling...what colour were they?... now steel grey, now midnight blue, now enigmatic black, and their owner as elusive in her character.

Such a beauty, her gown of deep blue revealed a sky blue underskirt and the silver silk puffed through the slashes in her sleeves which were so broad at the wrist they swept down to the floor. Her bodice was embroidered with moons and stars in gold and silver thread. She wore a circle of sapphires around her creamy neck and another crowned her dark hair which she had drawn back into a snood of silver lace.

She might indeed have been a moon goddess, a spirit of the season's pagan past.

However she was not. Her style proclaimed her a lady of France. She was the wife of that country's ambassador. Her outward appearance was all elegance and delightful charm but the one eye appraised her with prior knowledge of her activities both inside and outside the Courts of Europe as an adventuress and spy.

The one eye belonged to a Portuguese knight Sir Pedro Vacz de Cogna whose fine rapier with a jewelled hilt had earned him the title "the finest swordsman in Europe" for he was a notorious dueller and rarely left the field without leaving his opponent lying on it.

It was in the course of a duel that he had lost his other eye but famously had gone on to win the bout.

He was tall and seemingly over-slight with a thin face and delicate features that may have made him an unlikely warrior in another age but he was tough and wiry his arms and legs well-muscled and he had a long reach and fast reactions which made him a devil with a *coup de grace*.

His light weight gave him the agility of a dancer and his height an advantage over most of his opponents. The faint duelling scar on one cheek as well as the leather patch over his eye showed he was no stranger to violence and the other male guests stepped round him carefully so as not to bump against him and give offence.

Nevertheless he was courtly and well versed in the arts both of love and diplomacy and as it was a party he was not wearing his sword but had left it in the armoury with the other weapons.

Besides it was clear he had eyes only for the lady dressed like midnight.

There was that in the lady's eyes that declared she would not be averse to making his further acquaintance so by a long and circuitous route making many protestations of friendship along the way so as not to make his intentions too obvious he reached the side of Countess Emilie de Charolais.

Madame had for the moment lost her husband. M. le Comte was an elderly man, scholarly and amiable, who recognized the talents of his pretty arch wife and knew better than to encumber her at a party. He had wandered off to talk about books with the Bishop of St Albans, another elderly bibliophile.

Emilie de Charolais was shrewd and calculating. She knew her worth and counted her assets. Exquisite porcelain beauty and raven black hair, graceful movements, she could dance and sing divinely, spoke several languages and was as well-read as she was well-dressed. She drew all eyes towards her and she was well aware her warm femininity exerted a powerful charm.

The men she chose to wrap in her embraces would do anything for her and whisper any secrets into her pillow. Later she would tell her husband everything she had learnt.

He was, he said, too old for her preferring to spend his time with like-minded scholars and leave his wife to her own devices. He would take no offence at her amours provided she conducted herself discreetly which she always did. Thus he gave carte blanche to the many young men who fell in love with her although she was careful only to encourage those who were useful to her cause.

Sir Pedro knew all this. He had had first-hand experience of the lady's charms. Frankly he had made a great fool of himself and only extricated himself from scandal and ruin with the greatest difficulty.

Nevertheless being an adventurer himself he recognized a kindred spirit and bore no grudge. It had been an exhilarating passion and he had been a fool with his eyes wide open.

It was in defence of her honour that he had lost one of them.

Honour!

He smiled fondly at the memory. He retained a sneaking admiration for his cunning adversary.

She stood before him now the personification of all the Graces, elegant in her gown of midnight blue damask with its underskirt of silk the shade of a summer sky. It rustled seductively as she moved towards him and it crossed his mind that he would not mind reliving those heady days of passion and even as the thought crossed his mind it added: Fool! If only men could see her soul they would not be so enamoured with her. She is a dark goddess. An angel of death.

But she did not look like an angel of death now. Her features were softened by the firelight, her smile inviting and his eyes dropped to the little covering of lace at her bodice, a wisp of fragile armour to protect her inviting bosom.

He bowed and kissed her proffered hand chivalrously.

"Forgive lady, the presumption of a man with one eye but had I a pair I dare swear they would be equally dazzled by your beauty."

She dimpled at the compliment.

"Dear friend!" she purred. "How pleasant to find you in this company! I had thought to be bored but now I find I will be amused after all."

"Not by the mere sight of me I hope Madam nor by the memory of our previous acquaintance."

She did not even blush.

"The sight of you is one for sore eyes. You are a handsome dog and with so fine and careless a wit what lady would not find you amusing? I hear of few."

He accepted the accusation as just. He liked to think of himself as a ladies' man.

"There are many fine fellows here. I trust the dinner is not as overdressed."

"They are Spaniards. Spanish men are interested only in themselves. Flemings are only interested in money and the English are only interested in getting drunk. I tell you Sir Pedro I had every expectation of feeling very lonely tonight. You and I, French and Portuguese, are outside the alliance so no-one will wish to speak to us at all I dare say."

Sir Pedro noted that she was aware he was invited as the envoy of the King of Portugal although he had not mentioned that he was there in an official capacity. So she did know he was coming.

"What do you think of this alliance?"

Emilie de Charolais shrugged as if she did not consider such matters at all. She was a woman. What did a woman know about politics?

He laughed.

"Come Emilie. You can give me your husband's opinion. You must have heard him speak of it."

Emilie sighed as if it was all too much for her pretty little head.

"I believe our King and yours would be happy to see it fall."

So, thought Sir Pedro, that's why she is here. Not to see you, you fool!

They moved across to a position where no-one else could overhear them for the choir had just launched into a jubilant *Gaudeamus Igitur* a carol which is sung *fortissimo*.

As she was a foot shorter than him Sir Pedro was forced to bend his neck until he could feel her breath on his cheek. A surge of excitement raced through him. Damn it all man, keep your mind on the job!

"The Prince of York is prisoner in this house."

"Is he now?"

He tried to make no show of being interested but in truth he was very interested indeed.

"His incarceration is the price of the marriage contract. We have for months been intercepting diplomatic letters which referred to "the Condition" but it is only now that we discover what that condition is. The Spanish King has had him abducted in Scotland and surrendered him to English Henry. So now the alliance is sealed."

"Nothing we can do then."

Emilie looked reproachful.

"There is always something we can do. What if he were to escape...?"

Sir Pedro considered the likelihood. There were a few Spanish Guards, he had noted them in the courtyard. It was a common habit of his on entering any great house to count the men-at-arms just in case he needed to make a speedy getaway although now he was the Portuguese Envoy he reminded himself that should not be necessary. The Ambassador could not bring a large train of armed guards through the streets of London without attracting hostile attention. The Londoners were very prickly about armed gangs roaming their streets ever since they had been outlawed by their King. He only had three men with him but was confident of their abilities.

"Do we know where they are taking him?"

"The Tower."

"How do you know?"

"They came by water. They will leave the same way. They cannot row downriver to the Tower until after midnight."

"How do you know?"

"The tide my dear. The Thames is a tidal river. The tide will not turn until midnight."

"We could take them at the Watergate. Seize the Prince before he is put on board and be away through the park before anyone realizes. Daring but could be done. He will only have a few men around him as they put him in the boat."

"How do you know?"

"Too many and the boat will overturn."

Sir Pedro smiled a self-satisfied smile. In some areas he was an expert.

To acknowledge this fact Emilie traced his smile with her finger. It was a gesture that seemed to melt the marrow in his bones.

"His Majesty will be so grateful. He will want to see that you are adequately rewarded."

So, Sir Pedro reflected, would his own Sovereign. Portugal was looking askance on this alliance between Spain and England. Had she not her own eye on colonies in the New World?

All in all it looked like a night of rare opportunity.

He resolved to enjoy it to the full.

Chapter Eleven

Miles the Magician

Following his discussions with the Cardinal and the Flemish Ambassador Henry Medwall went in search of Miles Bloomfield.

He took him to one side and asked him confidentially, "Miles do you have about you a sleeping draught or could you make one within the hour?"

"I have a cornucopia of quackery but if you require an elixir with such alacrity I assume you are not the gentleman destined for the Land of Nod. We have a performance within the hour," responded the other genially, for despite his outward character which was a mixture of bombast and self-defence Miles Bloomfield was not slow on the uptake.

Henry pulled him a little further behind the pillar.

"It is for another party."

"Ha-ha! So when you say a sleeping draught what you are really desirous of obtaining is a tincture that will mix so adroitly with say a cup of spiced wine as to be both tasteless and odourless yet such as will in short order deliver to this other party a recumbentibus?"

"Alright Miles, I need knock-out drops. Can you supply me?"

"I am a wizard of the first water, a nonpareil among necromancers, a Doctor of Driromancy and Scatomancy, a conjuror withal famous for my light fingers. May one enquire as to the identity of this other party?"

"Peter Warbeck the viol player with the Flemish musikaaners."

"Poor Perkin! What can he have done?"

"Nothing. It is not for his fault that I must drug him but for his likeness."

Miles was not a playwright for nothing.

"I smell a plot! I smell a conspiracy!"

"Keep your voice down. You know why the ladies are in your company."

"Of course."

"With God's help when Lady Katharine boards her ship tonight she will not be alone."

"You mean to...?"

"Switch the simple servant for the Prince."

"Ah Terence thou should'st be living now!" declaimed Miles then by a deft piece of legerdemain he produced from the folds of his jerkin a small blue flask.

"A long list of holy and hard-hitting ones have by this divine restorative been kept sustenated, fortified, corroborated and consoled. There is nothing improves a man's temper like a good sleep be he bailiff, creditor or Undersheriff of the Shire provided that in the period between sleeping and waking the named defendant can put between his own person and the sweet somnambulist an equitable distance."

"Undersheriff?"

"A man must owe a trifle to his tailor," observed Miles unperturbed.

"How long will he sleep for?" inquired Henry keeping to the business in hand.

"How long do you need?"

"We need at least until midnight when they will wake him to take him to the Tower. They cannot leave earlier on account of the tide. So what? Five hours?"

Miles considered the timetable.

"He will sleep for four or five hours in a stentorian stupor after which on waking he will be stumbling and incoherent with no recollection of who he is, where he is or how he came there until he has slept again until tomorrow midday."

"They will get no sense out of him?"

"If he had any which I understand is debatable."

"They will think he is drunk."

"If he stinks of drink which can easily be arranged. Indeed he will believe he is drunk and go on to live a life of such continence and sobriety as will be to the great improvement of his character and the advantage of his soul."

Having thus disposed of the method they were forced to adjourn as the guests were now assembling in the hall and it was near the hour for the play to begin.

"When we break for dinner," Henry whispered as they returned to the tiring-rooms, "you must seek out Peter Warbeck and administer the drug. Take Tom and William with you. You will need to bring him down to the cellar as soon as he is senseless. John and I will deal with the guards."

Miles tapped his nose.

"I have the plot my dear *usque ad minimum quadrantum.* I am apprised to the minutest particle.

Indeed I believe it may be one of my own."

"Not a word Miles. Not now or in the future."

"Not even in the guise of a satire? I am a very Juvenal when I turn the point of my rapier wit upon the body politic. A hit here! Here touché!

"Not. A. Word."

"Mumchance then. I am the very soul of discretion. Fear me not! What part I play in this excellent conspiracy none shall ever know though many may guess and bless me for it."

Henry shook his head. Miles was incorrigible.

It was the very word for him. He had invented it.

Chapter Twelve

A dangerous co-incidence

When everything was ready Father Christmas with a borrowed trumpet called the guests to order and summoned the pages to usher them into the hall.

The Countess of Charolais contrived to ensure that she was seated next to the Portuguese envoy to the great pleasure of Sir Pedro who settled down to thoroughly enjoy a night of intrigue and adventure.

The hall was of the usual dimensions for a large refectory with a dais at the far end on which stood the High Table with its much-admired new Salt.

The Yule Log that had earlier been dragged into the fireplace was now blazing and candles had been lit in sconces all around the room to bathe the tables in flickering light greatly flattering to the beauty of an already lovely woman.

The hall was panelled and, as we noted earlier, decorated in fine style with boughs of holly and ivy and all manner of dried fruits and flowers so the scent of oranges, cinnamon, cloves and pine cones as well as great bowls of fragrant lavender and rose petals imparted a delicious aroma that hovered just above an even more delicious aroma of roasting meat drifting up from the kitchens below.

Along either side of the hall were set the great refectory tables with chairs along one side only so that the diners could watch the performance that was to take place in the centre of the hall between the tables.

Already as the guests were being seated the servants and retainers not invited to dine in the Great Hall were crowding in to stand behind the chairs and fill the corners because everyone wanted to see the play.

At the end of the Hall opposite the dais was an elaborately carved and painted screen depicting a small classical temple, a rustic landscape peopled by dancing Naiads and Dryads and to one side peeping around a gnarled and twisted olive tree a Satyr (or 'Satire'), a goat legged faun with horns and a tail his features exaggerated to give him a slightly devilish character but no-one who knew him could fail to spot the likeness as that of the Master of the Revels, the playwright Henry Medwall.

It was an in-joke which those who did know him fully appreciated and were eager to point out to those who had never seen the dramatist.

At that end of the hall were two doors to allow one set of servants to enter with full plates and one to exit with empty ones for the waiting at a banquet of this size and importance had to be organized with military precision. The same entrances would be used by the Players to make their entrances and exits so the screen was drawn across in front of them to keep them from view until they stepped out onto the area reserved for the 'stage'.

Immediately above them the minstrels sat in their gallery invisible to begin with being somewhat crowded out by the choir who had processed to the gallery to conclude their anthems.

As they reached the end of their performance and began filing out the professional musicians took over.

Sir Pedro glancing up at them suddenly gasped.

"What is it?" asked Emilie seeing something had grabbed his attention.

"That musician, the viol player. He was once one of mine. He was in my consort at my house in Lisbon for about a year."

"How does he come to be here? These men are wearing the livery of the Flemish Ambassador."

Sir Pedro shrugged.

"He is a Fleming although his mother is Portuguese, a woman of Faro. That's how he came to be recommended to my service. Her father had been a servant of my family for many years. He told me of his grandson's exceptional gifts. And indeed, my lady, if Peter Warbeck is to sing for us tonight we are in for a treat. He has a voice like liquid silver."

"You must have been very sorry to lose him."

"Ah lady, when it comes to musicians we noblemen are notable poachers. He was stolen from me by the Earl of Kildare who offered him twice what I was paying. At the time my pockets were to let and I could not afford to keep him so he went away to Dublin. I presume he must have returned to his native Tournai since and entered the service of the Flemish Ambassador."

"Well Sir Knight," purred the pliant Countess, "if his voice is all you say between his love-songs and your address I can see that my senses will be under assault this evening. How shall I be able to resist?"

“Not at all Madame I hope,” murmured Sir Pedro *sotto voce*.

She tapped him lightly on the chin.

“Behave yourself Sir. If his voice does not disappoint you tonight perhaps I may bid for his service and make him a present to you, provided our enterprise flourishes.”

Sir Pedro’s hopes soared.

Despite his ferocious and aggressive character he was a man of artistic sensibility who loved music above all other entertainments. Another man would not have recalled a boy musician who spent twelve months in his household but Sir Pedro admired talent. A gifted musician was a treasure to be coveted like any other conferring status on a gentleman marking him as a man of taste and giving him the opportunity to issue invitations to the most influential people at Court. He would rather be paid with the services of this musician than with a bag of gold.

For this reason when he could drag his one eye from the enticing undulations of his lady's bosom he kept it on Peter Warbeck who, unconscious of the interest being taken in his future, sang as the angels must have sung to the shepherds on the night of the first Christmas to another young man born under a travelling star.

As the applause died away the trumpet sounded. A drum-roll. Another fanfare. Silence everybody!

The clatter of conversation dropped to a murmur and then died away altogether.

The last throng of spectators crowded into the room and squeezed themselves in just inside the doors on either side of the screen.

Silence everybody!

Ssh!

The play is about to begin.

Chapter Thirteen

Fulgens and Lucres - Part One

Among the crowd of servants who have just piled into the Hall are two dressed so extravagantly that even in that room stuffed with extravagant fashions they stand out.

Imagine if you will parti-coloured hose, short tunics quilted and puffed fit to burst, enormous cod-pieces of tooled and gilded leather, shoes with such ridiculously long pointed toes they have to be gathered up by a chain and fastened just below the knees which make them walk with a strange loping stride to avoid tripping over their toes and the hats!

You have never seen such enormous hats adorned with bands and feathers and heaven knows what.

They appear to be part of the crowd but those who know their theatre recognize them at once. They are two of the most famous actors in London, playwrights both, Henry Medwall and Miles Bloomfield. The audience settles back to enjoy the show. They know they are in for some fun.

The two servants, known only as A and B because the playwright could not be bothered to think up names for them, open proceedings.

"Shall here be a play?" asks Servant A (Henry Medwall).

"Yes, for certain," responds Servant B (Miles Bloomfield).

"By my troth," says Servant A, "thereof I am glad and fain,

If you will believe me,

Of all the world I love such sport.

It gives me much pleasure and comfort

And causes me ever to resort

Where such a thing is put on.
I believe you yourself are one
Of those who shall perform?"
"No," protests B, "I am none.
I take it you are speaking in scorn
And taking..making fun."
"Ho!" declares A. "I thought by your fancy pants
You were a player."
B: Not a chance.

By this time, despite B's protestations to the contrary, the audience, even those unfamiliar with the two stars, will have divined from the intricate rhyme of their speech that these two are indeed players – Henry Medwall and Miles Bloomfield creating a famous double act – and that by this clever dramatic device they are about to begin the prologue.

Miles goes on to outline the story that they are about to tell which is as follows.

Once upon a time in the days of the Roman Empire there lived a noble

Senator whose name was Fulgens. He was renowned not just for his own wisdom and the virtuous character he had acquired in long years of public service but also for the beauty and goodness of his daughter Lucretia, or Lucres.

She had now reached the age where Fulgens was anxious to arrange for her a suitable marriage. Because of her spotless reputation all manner of young men were anxious to offer themselves as her suitors, many of them above her station in life who were willing to trade a large dowry in return for her beauty and renown.

Finally Fulgens whittled their number down to two. These were a young nobleman, Publius Cornelius and Gaius Flaminius. The two men were complete opposites. The Cornelian family was one of the most ancient in Rome and Publius Cornelius was therefore an aristocrat of the highest order. A dashing young man about town he had given his life up to the pursuit of pleasure relying on his family's good name and fortune for his status in Rome.

Gaius Flaminius on the other hand was a man of relatively humble origins who had risen in society due to his own great merits to the point where his fellow Romans held him in such respect they had appointed him Consul and as such he held one of the highest offices in the Empire.

Here the players pause to make their apologies for their theme is a politically sensitive one.

On the one hand it is complimentary to the Host for Cardinal Morton has risen from relatively humble origins to the second highest position of authority in the kingdom.

On the other there are present many representatives of the old aristocratic families who resent King Henry's attempt to transform England from an aristocracy, bearing in mind that for the past hundred years the country has been torn apart by constant feuds between these old aristocratic families, to a meritocracy in which men of talent from whatever background can rise to be of service to the state.

It is only because he has the patronage of a man as powerful as the Archbishop of Canterbury that Henry Medwall is able to express such a revolutionary view as to suggest merit might be valued more highly than an accident of birth.

The playwright's own apology is reinforced by the appearance of Fulgens himself who appears in both his manner and costume to resemble one of the ancient prophets or a venerable pope and sermonizes at length on the true spirit of the occasion which marks the birth of a Saviour who "letteth his sun shine on rich and poor" before coming to the point and outlining the arrangements he is making to secure his daughter's betrothal.

So difficult was it to decide between the two suitors, the one a scion of one of the oldest aristocratic families in Rome and the other a man of sterling qualities, that the matter was referred to the Senate who pronounced in favour of Gaius Flaminius. However he was the older man and Fulgens was a fond father, so he resolved to leave it to his daughter to choose which of the two she preferred as a husband.

Publius Cornelius found it so inconceivable that anyone might be considered a better catch than him that he went at once to Fulgens to put this to him. His family pedigree was impeccable. He was himself young and handsome. How could Fulgens look any further for a son-in-law?

Nevertheless Fulgens insisted that it was only proper that he should allow his daughter to make the final choice. He was not so hard a father that he would make her marry anyone against her will so Cornelius must wait on her decision.

Cornelius was disappointed but determined to pursue his courtship and win the hand of the fair Lucres.

At which point Servant B – our own Miles Bloomfield – steps out of the crowd and announces that he will offer his services to the noble Cornelius.

Servant A tries to dissuade him and says he will spoil the play but B is determined and suggests that since A is also without a master he too should join in the fun and offer his services to the other suitor Gaius Flaminius.

They are interrupted by the arrival of the lovely Lucres which draws gasps of astonishment from the crowd because in the flickering shadows of the hall, the aura of firelight and candlelight, this 'boy' appears for all the world like a lovely young woman. The transformation is astonishing.

The gasp is followed by cheers as the hero, Gaius Flaminius, in the popular person of John English, the most famous actor in the realm, strides into the hall.

Despite obediently assuring her father that she would accept the suitor of his choice Lucres really preferred Gaius Flaminius whose heroic character and sensible outlook on life was much closer to her own than that of the handsome but dandified Cornelius who thought of nothing but his own pleasure.

While Publius Cornelius was seeking her father's consent his rival Gaius Flaminius was trying to persuade Lucres to accept him as her husband. He readily admitted that he was not cut out to play the young lover. He was not a man for fine words and pretty trinkets, but he promised Lucres that if she chose him he would always be faithful to her to the end of his days.

Lucres was touched by this assurance and divined from his promises that Gaius Flaminius was the better man because she was a young woman of good sense as well as virtuous character not to be tempted by jewels and pretty but meaningless compliments.

However she was also a woman so instead of confirming her attachment to him Lucres decided to make Gaius Flaminius wait for her decision which she claimed required her father's consent

Gaius Flaminius took his leave of her feeling rather disheartened. He did not know how else he could woo this lovely girl.

At which point Servant A steps out of the crowd and offers his services to this good man and upon a reference being duly provided by his friend B who vouches for him he is duly engaged and sent to try and persuade Lucres to accept his master's proposal.

Lucres had a pretty maidservant named Joan whom she used as a go-between. Cornelius' servant had been trying in vain to win her over but she was as sensible as her mistress and kept him dangling with promises but no more.

Lucres sent her with a message to Gaius Flaminius to give him encouragement as she secretly wished to make him her final choice. However she felt that she could not do so immediately as Publius Cornelius would be offended if she failed to treat his request with equal consideration so instead she sent Joan to seek out Gaius' servant to take a message to him to explain her intentions.

On meeting A Joan saw an opportunity to make her lover B jealous and perhaps bring him to the point of making a proposal of marriage.

On seeing Joan with his rival B flew into a rage of jealousy and challenged him there and then to a duel.

Since they were servants they were both unarmed so they had to make the most of what they had.

First they engaged in a singing competition but since neither of them could carry a tune in a bucket Joan soon put a stop to that.

Then they had the idea of a wrestling match but Joan declared it a draw.

Thirdly they decided on a joust using mops for lances and buckets on their heads for helmets. Craftily Joan suggested she tie their hands together to make it easier for them to hold their 'lances'.

They ran at each other and clashed so violently they both fell down. As they lay exhausted Joan found a piece of rope and tied them both up. Since neither of them had their hands free they could not escape. Having given them both a taste of their just desserts Joan skipped off and left them there where they were found a little later by Gaius Flaminius.

He untied them and called his servant back to his duty having realized that he had taken on a man of dubious reliability and demanded of him what message he had received from Lady Lucres.

A was contrite realizing he had found a fair and generous master so he reassured him by telling him that Lady Lucres had sent the following message.

She said she had arranged a meeting at which her father and Cornelius would both be present to see fair play and at that meeting she would allow her two suitors to present their case and on that basis she would make her decision.

Gaius Flaminius was not sure of his ability to win the argument for Publius Cornelius was a young man of honeyed words and smooth address. He had all the attributes of a courtier whereas he, Gaius, had none.

All he had to offer was his good nature, fond heart and steady character.

He was not sure that for a pretty young woman like Lucres this would be enough.

His servant encouraged him by telling him to go home and work on his defence and Gaius Flaminius took his leave.

At which point Servant A steps back into his role of Author to wind up the first part by pointing out that the guests are growing hungry and if they have to wait any longer for their dinner the Players will have outstayed their welcome.

With a flourish and a drum-roll Part One draws to a close.

The Players step aside to give entry to a small army of waiters who line up to clap in the Boar's Head held high by the Head Cook beaming broadly whose pride in his achievement is rewarded by the heartfelt applause of the noble company who are reminded that they are indeed beginning to feel hungry.

The Cardinal intones a short grace bearing in mind that the food is hot and the guests impatient.

The Boar's Head is set down on High Table and waiters begin to move into the intricate dance that they have rehearsed over and over again as plates are passed up the table, salvers are brought in with meat and vegetables, sauces and spices, side dishes and jugs of wine.

The guests settle themselves to enjoy their meal and Christmas dinner is ready to begin.

And where are the Players?

They vanished the moment the Boar's Head was brought in.

Chapter Fourteen

Prince and Pretender

Immediately they left the hall the Players split into two teams. Miles, Tom and William went to show English hospitality to the Flemish Ambassador's consort who had for the duration of the feast been relieved by the musicians of the Cardinal's own household and were resting in a side chamber adjacent to the gallery.

The ladies retired to their dressing room to avoid being too closely scrutinized while Henry and John English donned the livery of the Cardinal's bodyguard and hurried down to the cellar.

The prisoner was not being kept in the wine-cellar since the pages were running in and out of there keeping the guests liberally supplied but in a part of the cellar walled off from the main vault and furnished with a stout door to make it serviceable as a strong-room.

The door had a grille in it which admitted light and air, although not much of either, which allowed its secondary use as a temporary gaol.

It lay beyond a small antechamber with a brazier that provided the only warmth in this chilly part of the Palace and billowed smoke around the low vaulting and sturdy pillars behind which a man with a clandestine purpose might usefully hide.

However John and Henry took a more direct approach. They bowled in beaming with bonhomie and greeting the Spanish guards, two by the fire and one by the cellar door they noted carefully, with courteous bows and handshakes.

Henry explained in Spanish that they had come to relieve them so that they could go and join the feast.

Two of the guard were ready to leave immediately for despite the smoking fire in the brazier the damp atmosphere was a reminder that they were below the level of the river but the third man was punctilious in his duty and politely declined on behalf of them all saying they could not leave their charge unguarded.

"Pikestaff and pillage!" expostulated Master English getting into character. "Here is one of your "impossibility" men called in English a Jobsworth. Great Heaven Senor there is a fat roast goose awaiting your attention with vegetables, a savoury pudding or two and sweet sauces to tickle your nostrils and bring ecstasy to your palate for know the Cardinal has a very fine French Cook. Added to which there is a tun of sack to get your insides around."

The Spaniards struggled to follow his English but got the general idea quickly enough from the accompanying mime and the two who were cold and hungry attempted to persuade their sterner colleague

Even he was weakening at the mention of roast goose with fine sauces and as much sack as he could hold.

Henry, ever the diplomat, saw that victory was at hand and deftly delivered the *coup de grace.*

"Surely," he protested, "you cannot wish to insult our Lord by refusing his generosity. He was most insistent, personally insistent that you should not be left out of the feast and has set aside a room for your particular comfort. You must know that in England Christmas is the most important season of the year. It is the season when hospitality is king and to refuse it gives the gravest offence. He has even sent men of his own bodyguard to watch over the prisoner while you eat. You must know the saying "When in Rome do as the Romans do.""

He could not have chosen his argument more cogently for the

Spanish, even in the lower ranks, were obsessive in the matter of correct behaviour and the observation of niceties of rank so the soldier realized very quickly that it was imperative in him to show good manners and an appreciation of the honour granted to his dignity as an under-captain by the most illustrious of the English Lords and a Cardinal to boot who clearly recognized his worth.

Thus he good-naturedly handed over his sword and meekly followed his enthusiastic companions who were conducted by John English to the delights he had promised although they might have found it themselves by following their noses.

Henry quickly drew out the key the Cardinal had given him and unlocked the door to the store-room.

The Prince lay huddled in the straw wrapped in his cloak against the cold apparently in a dead sleep but he had been listening carefully to what was going on outside and when he saw Henry his face lit up and he was quickly restored to life and action.

"Quickly Sir," Henry urged him. "We do not have much time."

As he spoke there was a scraping sound outside the door and the squeaking of wheels on the uneven paving.

The Prince stepped swiftly back and resumed his position slumped on the floor with his cloak over him. Henry cautiously closed the door and stood stock-still in the shadows behind it the guardsman's sword in his hand.

He took a careful peek through the grille and saw that John English had sunk back into the shadows behind the pillar, his sword also drawn in case of necessity.

Through the doorway came a large wicker hamper, one of those used by the players to stow their costumes, pushed by the indefatigable Master Miles with Tom and William in tow.

Henry sighed with relief and stepped out of the cell.

"Come, Highness," he said to the Prince. "You are among friends."

The Prince scrambled to his feet and followed him out into the antechamber.

"Where is the musician?"

Miles pointed to the hamper.

"It seemed the easiest way to get him down the corridor without anyone asking questions."

Tom and William lifted the lid of the wicker basket and hauled out the inert body of the young Fleming.

Glancing from his pale face to the almost equally white face of the Prince Henry saw at once that the likeness was a very good one. As long as Peter Warbeck did not speak, or at least not coherently, for the next five hours they would get away with it.

Henry signalled to the Prince to remove his clothes and they hurriedly dressed the musician in them wrapped him in the Prince's cloak and laid him tenderly on the straw in the store-room half-buried his face well-covered by the hood as the Prince had been.

He seemed comfortable enough and was left to snore as peacefully as a baby.

When they were all out Henry locked the door from the outside and pocketed the spare key. The senior Spanish guard, who he had to admire for his forethought, had taken the other key with him to be on the safe side.

Just as well Henry thought that I had my forethought before him.

The Prince in his underclothes shivering in the damp air of the antechamber asked "What about me?"

Now followed a masterpiece of theatrical transformation.

From inside the hamper Miles produced a magnificent paunch a real beer belly of feathers and down which he strapped to the Prince's lithe person completely changing his shape.

Tom and William set about with a tin of blacking to change his nationality and added a pair of fierce eyebrows and a bushy beard.

As a finale they draped him in a robe of cloth of gold with an emerald surcoat and a scarlet turban fixed with a brooch of such splendid rubies and emeralds that if it were not paste it would have been worth a fortune.

"Am I not a trifle conspicuous?" mused the Prince regarding the bright colours of his costume and the gaudy jewellery.

"Not in the company you will be keeping," Henry assured him, "and the magnificence of your costume will enhance your disguise. No-one will be looking for a fugitive in such eye-catching apparel. They will look for someone imitating a shadow. Those who do mark you will notice your costume and not your person. People seldom notice the actor inside the mask. Invisibility is all about letting people see what they expect to see."

Knowing Henry's talent for espionage Prince Richard wisely accepted his word and allowed the players to do what they knew best. They adjusted his costume until to their eyes it was perfect and he would pass without question as a Moor of Spain.

Lastly Miles presented him with a scimitar and drawing it from its scabbard showed him that it was no cardboard toy.

"In case of need," he whispered, "best go armed."

A slender dagger, also a genuine stiletto and no plaything, was slipped into his belt.

Miles stood back to admire his handiwork.

"I can find no fault," he said with some satisfaction. "His own mother would not recognize him."

In this guise Tom and William led him away to mingle among the Mummers and become lost in the crowd.

Miles remained for he had bought a couple of other useful props, a flagon and an empty bottle of brandy-wine.

"Our musician had the rest of it," he said apologetically. "My but these Flemings have hard heads. They might as well be Englishmen."

He and John sat themselves down on the seats beside the fire vacated by the two guards and all three waited their nerves as taut as the strings on Peter Warbeck's viol.

It seemed an age before the guards returned as full of good cheer as they had been short of it half an hour earlier.

There was a great deal of slapping of backs and shaking of hands as they endeavoured to express their appreciation of England's favourite holiday.

The punctilious one nevertheless remembered to look in on the prisoner who was fast asleep.

He tried the door. It was locked fast.

Satisfied he turned away.

"He sleeps like the dead," he observed cheerfully.

Miles looked apologetic.

"Dead drunk I fear. I offered him a tankard through the bars with the compliments of the season meaning him to keep it to drink with his dinner but he downed the whole in the time it took to sing him a carol. Brandy-wine. Very strong."

He opened the flagon and let the guard sniff the strong spirit it had once held. The guard drew back at the first whiff.

"Ha!" he exclaimed in halting English, "you English can drink."

"At least," said Henry consolingly, "he won't give you any trouble and it will keep him from catching cold."

This cheered the guards even more. They were all for an evening without any trouble.

The English clapped them on the back again and wished them a Merry Christmas then handing back their weapons left them to resume their monotonous duty.

They had just time to race up to their dressing rooms and reassume their characters for the play when the major domo came to announce that the tables were being cleared and the players would shortly be expected back in the hall.

"One minute gentlemen!"

One minute!

As his footsteps receded down the corridor the fanfare was sounded in the hall.

Chapter Fifteen

A close Call

An account of what followed was published in 1509 by William Rastell's brother John who faithfully recorded everything that happened during this historic performance. That the book survived is perhaps explained by the fact that the manuscript is inscribed *"I am Miles Blomefyldes booke"* for if Miles kept his word and kept mum he made sure that some clue as to his part in the adventure was passed down to posterity.

The fanfare warning the audience to look sharp, take their seats and settle down was followed by the usual drum-roll.

There was a slight anticipatory pause as the audience waited for the performance to resume.

The pause went on a little longer than was strictly comfortable so the trumpeter stepped into the breach and repeated the fanfare, a little more loudly so that it could be heard along the corridor in the tiring rooms.

Another pause.

The audience was beginning to shuffle. Had something gone wrong? The trumpeter took another deep breath.

Just as he was putting his lips to the mouthpiece Henry Medwall burst into the room slightly out of breath and still buttoning the riotously embroidered tunic he was wearing as Servant A.

Stumbling into the centre of the hall he adjusted his codpiece to a general shout of laughter and greeted his impatient audience with a hasty improvisation.

“Much good it will do you each and every one.

You will not believe how fast I have run
For fear that I should be late!
No sweat! Just a little perspiration
Have I lost to serve your delectation –
May my cold courage now abate!

(And they had no idea how heartfelt that last line was)

But now to the matter I came for..."

And he was back with the script.

Thus neatly excusing his tardy appearance, and making it seem yet another casual dramatic device he moved on effortlessly to a lengthy summary of the First Act partly to remind the audience where they had got to in the plot and partly to give his colleagues more time to collect themselves and be ready and waiting in the wings.

As he finally dried up Miles made his appearance as Servant B also apologizing for his apparent tardiness thus making it seem more than ever that Henry's delayed appearance was merely a plot device in the play. B's excuses were swiftly overlooked because he had come to introduce that indispensable feature of any Yuletide entertainment the arrival of the Mummers here worked into the play as an interlude hired by the handsome Cornelius to please the Lady Lucres while they awaited the arrival of Fulgens and Gaius Flaminius to hear her choice of suitor.

However nothing succeeds in the theatre like suspense.

Instead of bringing on the Mummers Cornelius delayed their entrance by asking B to beg him a few moments' conversation with his lady sending her a token as a reminder of a romantic walk they had shared in the garden.

Miles took this opportunity to demonstrate his gift for slapstick comedy delivering the token with a mixture of ineptitude and slow cunning and embarking on a series of elaborate fart jokes without which then as now no English pantomime could ever be considered complete.

Such vulgar low comedy convulsed the audience but appeared to shock the virtuous Lucres who correctly divined the true interpretation of Cornelius' message showing herself to be indeed a young woman of pure mind and superior intellect. Accordingly she permitted the ardent Cornelius to have a private word.

Alas it availed him nothing as she still continued to insist she would not give her decision until Gaius Flaminius was also present.

Nothing for it then.

Bring on the dancers.

Now came the long-awaited Disguising.

Ah if only the audience knew how true that was.

As the spectacle unfolded the players collectively held their breath.

At the head of the procession came the Spanish dancers resplendent in their flamenco costumes, swirls of red and gold ruffles, yards of black lace, tapping in time to their castanets all elegance and exciting rhythm. The Spanish Ambassador appreciating the compliment to his nation immediately burst into applause and everyone else followed suit.

Behind them came the consort of famous musicians fresh from Flanders. Twisting and turning among the dancers it would take a sharp eye to notice there were only five of them.

It took only one.

“Wait!” rang out the voice of the Portuguese envoy leaping to his feet. “Why are there only five? Where is Peter Warbeck?”

For a moment the actors froze. Lucres showed an unwonted affection for Cornelius by grasping the actor’s hand and clutching it tightly.

It took a true professional, a trouper of the first order, to grab the attention of the puzzled audience.

Miles' instinct as an actor did not fail him.

Lurching into the line of dancers with the clumsy grace of a natural clown he performed a ballet of tipsy tumbling crying in a thick Flemish accent: "Marry! As for one of them his lip is sore. He cannot blow a pipe, he is so sick!"

Without abandoning his character he mimed a drunken stagger and what is known in England as "brewer's droop" which got a huge laugh not least from the Flemish Ambassador because the Flemings were throughout Europe nearly as famous for their heavy drinking as the Anglo Saxons.

Also the Flemish Ambassador knew why Peter Warbeck was not there.

If he was not there the plan had succeeded.

He stood up himself and made a pantomime of enjoying the joke taking everyone's eyes off the Portuguese envoy who was encouraged by his neighbour, the Countess of Charolais, to sit down and applaud the comedian. Obviously it was all part of the show.

Miles continued to entertain and play his part dancing in and out of the line of performers conducting and tumbling by turns making his act as much part of the show as possible.

"Spiel up tambourine! Ich bid owe frelike!"

Henry, seeing him thus exposed hurried on the rest of the Mummers and the moment was lost in Oohs and Aahs as the audience was dazzled by the gorgeous costumes and extraordinary contortions of the troupes of dancers.

Masked in gold and black they displayed every example of finery, furs, feathers, ruffs, embroidery, and all the wonderful fabrics produced in England and the Netherlands, silks, satins, velvets figured and plain, damask and tapestry.

Imagine the effect of this in the flickering candlelight and firelight, how they glittered and glistened and shimmered by turns and appeared so fantastic and phantasmagoric as to realize a dream.

Representing Spain and Flanders the two lines of dancers paraded around the hall then joined hands representing their respective alliances with England and began a stately Sarabande which then gave way to a performance of wild Spanish dancing in the gypsy style to exhilarating unfamiliar rhythms.

However Sir Pedro continued to stand looking everywhere for his young protégé. Surely he was not really drunk on this most important night of the year?

Another band of dancers entered the room, all in red, green and gold.

Lucres, following the script, asked Miles where these dancers were from.

“Are these from Wales?” she enquired.

The answer that should have come back was “No, they’re the wild Irish.”

Seeing Sir Pedro still standing up and drawing attention to himself Miles engagingly turned the compliment and directed it at the envoy by announcing instead “No, they are the Portugales.”

John Rastell recording the performance inadvertently recorded both the original line in the book and the line that was actually spoken on that night so that it reads “No they’re the wild Irish Portugales” which makes no sense.

But on the night it not only made sense but drew great applause and turned all eyes on the Portuguese Envoy who had no choice but to take a bow and accept the compliment graciously.

Feeling slightly foolish Sir Pedro sat down and the parade of Mummers swept on past him as they circled the space in the centre of the great hall, dancing, singing, bowing to the guests as they passed them, a riot of music, costume and colour.

Gradually the Mummers concluded their dances, sang their final round and passed in a stately fashion out of the Great Hall and the actors were able to get down to the serious business of concluding the Argument.

When Fulgens and Gaius Flaminius had arrived at the appointed place the lady Lucres and Publius Cornelius were already there watching some dancers performing a masque. When the dancing had finished and the last strains of the music died away Fulgens called them all to order and announced that the two suitors would each put their case and the lady Lucres would then make her decision as to which one would be her choice as a husband.

Because his aristocratic lineage gave him the higher rank Publius

Cornelius demanded that he be heard first.

He painted a picture in words of his noble ancestry and the great deeds of his forbears who had been among the founders of Rome. He was their descendant and their blood ran in his veins. But in the end all his argument boiled down to was that a woman can desire nothing more than a husband of a wealthy and aristocratic family. His lineage alone should be enough to satisfy Lucres.

Then it was the turn of Gaius Flaminius.

Apologising for his insolence for he was deeply conscious of his comparatively humble birth he argued that Cornelius relied too much on the achievements of his ancestors. While they had indeed been instrumental in creating the Roman Republic he had not devoted his own talents to public service. Indeed while he boasted much of his ancestors' good deeds he could not boast of any good deeds of his own. He had spent his life in dissipation and the frivolities of fashion.

His behaviour was anything but noble. The gist of Gaius' argument might be distilled into the English proverb "Handsome is as handsome does." Cornelius was undoubtedly handsome in his person but his character left much to be desired.

He, Gaius Flaminius, on the other hand had risen entirely as a consequence of his own merits and good character and had earned his right to high office and the respect of his fellow men.

Lucres had already made up her mind but she didn't wish to humiliate either of her suitors by rejecting one in front of the other for she was a kind-hearted girl and careful of other people's feelings.

Instead she insisted that she had listened to them both very carefully and she would respond to each of them privately.

When the gentlemen had withdrawn she called the servant of Gaius Flaminius to her and told him that she wished him to convey a message to his master that she had chosen him for his many good qualities over the wealth and nobility of Publius Cornelius for she believed Gaius Flaminius was by his nature the nobler man.

To which Servant B responded cheekily but not unreasonably that she could tell him herself.

So the play in spite of its rude knockabout comedy and gaudy spectacle did at last turn out to be a morality play fit for performance in the Cardinal's Hall.

"...and that done of all this play," concluded Henry Medwall with a deep respectful bow to the Cardinal, "..shortly here we make an end."

Whereupon after receiving the thanks and acknowledgement of the Cardinal and the great applause of his guests the players quit the stage.

Chapter Sixteen

Sir Pedro smells a rat

Sir Pedro Vasc de Cogna had sat brooding ever since the start of the second act.

While the other guests around him were discussing, some quite vociferously, the merits of the argument that meritocracy is better than aristocracy he stayed in his seat his brow furrowed and his brandy untouched before him.

“Why Sir Pedro,” exclaimed the Countess soothing his wrinkled forehead, “this brown study? Surely you are not still concerned about the fate of your missing musician? I dare say he is in the kitchens now carousing with the rest of the servants."

Sir Pedro could not let it go.

"Surely," he worried, "he would not get so drunk as to miss this important performance. I know this Warbeck. He is simple but conscientious. He loves music and is very obedient to his calling."

"This English Christmas is a great occasion for drink," observed the Countess matter-of-factly. "There will be as many sore heads as shriven souls tomorrow."

Sir Pedro acknowledged the truth of this and yet he was not satisfied.

To be sure Master Bloomfield's adept ad lib and energetic clowning had made it all seem part of the act but why had Peter Warbeck not come in at the end and taken his bow with the others? His performance had been sterling. He surely deserved his share of the applause.

Perhaps he was indeed drunk or taken ill? He had never been inclined to drink to excess in the time

Sir Pedro had known him but back among his native Flemings it would be no wonder if he had succumbed to the traditions of his own countrymen.

Yet still Sir Pedro was not satisfied. As a swordsman he was a man as much guided by instinct as reason.

As the dinner crowd began to disperse into the antechamber to allow the hall to be cleared for dancing he leaned towards the Countess and whispered: "If we are to take the Prince tonight I had better go and check our path. It is always good to know where your exits are in case of trouble."

The Countess nodded as if she were just listening to a snippet of casual gossip.

"I should go and rejoin my husband," she said loudly for any bystanders to here. "The poor dear will be quite lost without me."

With a swish of her skirts she was gone.

Sir Pedro watched her go with an expression of wry regret and then wandered out into the corridor where a few guests were mingled with the Mummers, all the Spanish costumes so gorgeous it was difficult to tell them apart.

He strolled casually down the corridor as if he were just stretching his legs brushing past a fat Moor with a bushy beard to whom he paid no more attention than an empty suit of armour until he came to the entrance to the cellar which he had noted earlier from the presence of the Spanish guards.

He wandered down the stairs and into the main vault and looked around.

The door to the side chamber was ajar and there was a light within so he deduced this was being used as the guard-room.

The guards snapped to attention as soon as he entered but seeing that he was Portuguese and not a Spanish nobleman they relaxed a little.

"What can we do for your honour?" inquired the punctilious one cautiously.

"To see the prisoner."

"For what reason?"

"I am the Portuguese Ambassador. It is my duty to see fair play and to satisfy myself that he is well."

It seemed a reasonable excuse. He was alone and unarmed.

The guard shrugged and bade him look for himself.

Sir Pedro glanced through the grille. The prisoner lay in a pile of straw covered by a hooded cloak. He could not see his face.

"Is he not well?"

"Only drunk. The Englishmen gave him a mug of brandy-wine out of kindness to wish him the compliments of the season and the clot downed the lot. Only the English and Flemings would drink good wine by the mug-full. He is drowned in sweet oblivion worst luck as it means we will have to carry him to the boat. He is well enough," added the conscientious guard. “We have heard him snoring.”

“Englishmen?” Sir Pedro’s nerves tightened up at the word. Suddenly he was as wary as a cat.

“The English guards. The Cardinal’s men. They came to relieve us while we had our supper.”

Sir Pedro suppressed a thin smile. It was exactly what he would have done.

“I should like to see him more closely,” he insisted. “I need to see his face.”

The shrug was again eloquent but an under-captain does not argue with an Ambassador particularly one who has a reputation as the finest swordsman in Europe.

He unlocked the door and allowed De Cogna to enter.

Sir Pedro borrowed a candle and held it over the sleeping captive who did not stir. He knelt down beside him and lifted his hood.

It was as he thought.

No need to wonder further what had become of the innocent musician.

He uttered a malison – that is to say he swore violently but under his breath. He did not wish the guards to know he had noticed anything amiss.

If the Englishmen had the Prince they would get him away from the palace and by road. It would be easier to take him from them than tackle the guards on the water.

"The English you say gave him this drink?"

The guard nodded. "Irregular I know but you know how the English like their drink. And it being the season of goodwill… We were not here at the time or I should have prevented it."

"Of course. The Cardinal's men you say? Are you sure?"

"They were wearing his livery. Men of his personal bodyguard."

"Well, well. He seems peaceful enough. No harm done. It is a great season of hospitality in England.

They insist even a condemned man is entitled to his share of the feasting."

The guard looked wary. He seemed to be getting off the hook very lightly although of course De Cogna was a mere Portuguese. If he'd been a Spanish nobleman there would have been hell to pay.

Sir Pedro bade them farewell and accepted a smart salute from all three guards anxious to see the back of him.

As he turned away he spotted a small rosette of cloth of gold that had fallen beneath a bench.

Pretending to adjust his shoe he scooped it up. It did not come from his own suit nor any of the guards. Somehow he doubted that it was part of the Cardinal's livery.

Henry Medwall! The Cardinal's right-hand man and secret agent.

"I thank you for your patience," he said again to the guards. "I will report your good diligence to your master."

Thus leaving them satisfied he strode back through the cellar and ran up the stairs as quickly as he dared without making his need for speed too obvious.

In the corridor he collared a page.

“The Players!” he demanded. “Have they left yet?”

“Yes Sir,” said the little boy wriggling somewhat in his iron grip. “They left as soon as the play was done. You should have seen them singing and dancing and tumbling with all the Mummers round them. You could hear them clear across the park and all the torches blazing.”

Yes, thought Sir Pedro cynically, that was just the kind of stunt Medwall would pull to leave in plain sight.

“I am sorry to have missed it. Which way did they go?”

“Towards Southwark Sir.”

De Cogna released the child with a wolfish smile he fondly imagined was avuncular.

He stood for a moment wondering what to do. The Countess of Charolais came in search of him.

"That's a grim face for this merry occasion," she chided him. "What has happened?"

Sotto voce he quickly told her how he had confirmed his suspicions.

"The prisoner is Warbeck. They have contrived to switch him for the prince. He has escaped with the actors. Do we raise a hue and cry?"

The lady thought carefully.

"I think not. We do not know how far the Cardinal is involved. Do not arouse the guards. Let us tell no-one of our suspicions. They will deliver the musician to the Tower tonight. Tomorrow the deception will be discovered. That alone may be enough to break the accord if Henry is so minded. In the meantime let us stick to our plan. You go after the Prince and bring him back to our custody. We may still strike a useful bargain with him. You know where they have gone?"

"To Southwark the boy said."

"Eastwards, downriver then. To the sea. Have you enough men for this venture?"

The Portuguese Ambassador had only three but he was confident of their abilities and their discretion. His own reputation as a notable swordsman was without doubt.

"What shall we do then?"

"Bring him to our Embassy. We are lodged within the precincts of Westminster. There he may claim sanctuary and we may generously offer him our protection."

"That would be an advantage to France but not to Portugal. I was thinking of a ransom."

"The Dowager Duchess? That's a thought. She will pay handsomely to get her nephew back."

And I will see that she does thought Sir Pedro who was not a rich man. And I will see the Prince does not go anywhere near Westminster tonight. A Portuguese merchantman was tied up at Wapping loaded with English wool in exchange for wine. If his adventure was to meet with success that night the Prince would be on it and on his way to Lisbon before her ladyship got wind that she had been double-crossed.

"He cannot have gone far in that heavy wagon," he murmured half to himself. "The Mummers are on foot and they cannot outrun them without attracting suspicion. They will hold their nerve and move slowly. I will collect my sword from the armoury and my men and I will to horse and follow them."

"Seize the day my Pierrot," purred the lady enticingly. "Victory and fortune will be yours and I can promise you a reward at the end of it."

Sir Pedro laughed. He knew what sort of a reward she had in mind but he was older now, more mature he reminded himself, and kept his mind firmly on the cash.

He bowed curtly, kissed her hand like a true gallant and strode swiftly from the hall.

Ten minutes later he had strapped on his sword and was in the saddle with his three bodyguards and close companions alongside him.

He had tarried overlong with the Countess. The Players had cleared the park. There was no sign of the procession or their torches.

They trotted sedately out of the courtyard so not as to arouse any great interest in their going then kicked their heels into the flanks of their horses and spurred them to a gallop along the avenue of trees.

The Players had a head start but they had the faster horses.

They would catch them at The George.

Chapter Seventeen

The George, Southwark

Now our play is nearly ended and we must cut to the chase.

As the Portuguese men-at-arms galloped away from the Bishop's Palace and made swift strides across the open ground before they were forced to slow to a walk in the narrow crowded streets of Lambeth the Players who had of necessity been travelling at a slower pace turned into the courtyard of The George.

While they had been in progress a transformation had been taking place.

Queen Elizabeth and Katharine had abandoned their female characters entirely and taken advantage of their new roles as 'boys' to don the costume of foresters and were now indistinguishably masculine in their green serge jerkins and leather hoods provided they kept their hoods up and stayed out of the light.

Their boots and breeches meant they would find it easier to ride astride, Katharine to Greenwich with her husband and the Queen to Eltham where her children awaited her in expectation of presents and kisses from her on Christmas morning.

The Prince had removed his blacking and Moorish garb and had assumed the character of "Third Forester".

At Southwark the Mummers dispersed and fresh horses were procured to take Henry and the fugitives to Greenwich, he being needed to show them the road.

The other players were to remain at The George until he returned to assure them of the success of their night's work since too large a party might attract the notice of the constables who were very vigilant since the King had come down severely on large retinues.

The party was just preparing to mount up when the Portuguese Knight of the One Eye thundered into the yard with his trio of swordsmen.

Dismounting they strode across the cobbles.

"Hold you!" bawled De Cogna levelling his blade at the Prince. "You shall not escape this night Sir Rebel! I know who you are. You are to come with me."

The fugitives stood frozen to the spot. All that stood between the Prince, his good wife and the Queen of England and the sharp tips of the Portuguese swords were a quartet of actors.

"Regard them not," snapped Sir Knight dismissively. "They are mere players."

Such an insult was not to be supported.

Miles Bloomfield struck the attitude of Outrage!

"Regardez-vous," he mimicked him sarcastically strutting like a bantam cock. "We are no mere players. You are addressing the *lusores regis, inter alia, les playars of the King's Enteyrludes* trained in all the thespian arts. Know you we are proficient in high comedy, low comedy, tragedy and its inevitable concomitant farce, wrestling, tumbling, fisticuffs, quarterstaffs, lechery and archery, *Terpsichore..*" (here he executed a little jig) "...even those sports practiced by the God of Love, alchemy, astrology, conjuring and legerdemain, and above all...SWORDPLAY!"

On which cue all four players with the perfect timing born of long rehearsal drew together and took their guard.

"So then," continued Miles with ebullient confidence, "we can fence you in the English Style, the French, the Italian, the Spanish, the Russian, the Chinese ..you name it. You men of Portugal may consider yourselves fortunate that we English are blessed with an equitable temper for were you to put it to the critical judgement of these good people…" the galleries were already filling up with a very interested and appreciative audience "…whether or not the King's Players are not famed for their virility, their very potency *en cas de combat* you would receive from them a surety that any engagement between ourselves will certifiably result in an ambuscade of the auricular orifices."

His opponents looked baffled and not only because they were Portuguese.

Miles sighed.

"I hint at cuffing of ears."

This they understood and advanced with vengeful determination.

"Now then," interposed John English in a more conciliatory tone. "Can this not be decided between us as reasonable men?"

He raked them with his charm approaching the man nearest to him and extending his left hand winningly.

"Can we not make terms with a sweet little coaxing hand-kiss?"

As he lifted his left hand to shake that of his opponent he drew the man's uncertain gaze and raising his sword hilt with his right fetched him a thumping blow with his sword hilt driving him back upon the cobbles and sprawling him in the horse trough.

De Cogna hauled him out in a vicious temper.

"Enough!" he barked. "They are mountebanks and changelings. Have at them!"

"Gentlemen," observed Miles, for once succinctly, "Engage!"

Then it was all clashing of steel and the air rent with oaths and imprecations, scuffles and blows.

"Go Henry! Go!" cried John English parrying one blow and jumping out of the way of another. "We will hold them as long as we can."

The fugitives wasted no time in words but were quickly to horse and clattering out of the yard they swung to the east and the gallops of Blackheath.

The actors proved to be competent opponents. They had the advantage of numbers as the Queen stayed with them and proved no mean hand with a rapier. They were tricky, unconventional adversaries which made it difficult to second-guess their next move and they were not averse to cheating.

Nevertheless they were up against professionals led by a man whose reputation was feared throughout Europe. It was not to be supposed they could hold them for long.

In what seemed no time at all the Portuguese were able to fight themselves clear and back to their horses.

"Leave them," commanded De Cogna, "they are of no use to us. We must follow the Prince. He must not be allowed to get away."

The winded players could only watch helplessly as they leaped into the saddle and swept out of the courtyard following the same road as the others had taken.

"Nil desperandum!" cried John English when he had enough breath for a Player is never without hope.

He pointed to a light cart which stood by in the stable ready harnessed to two likely geldings.

He chivvied his company onto the cart leaped into the driving seat and taking the reins shook them with a "Giddyup!" and within a whisker of a minute had them bowling east on the trail of the vanishing horsemen.

"We'll never catch them," shouted Miles and they bumped and bounced onto a heathland track with never a rider in sight.

"Never fear!" yelled back John English veering down the left fork at the New Cross instead of the right signposted to Greenwich. "I know a short cut."

Chapter Eighteen

A Swift Caravel

As the chimes of midnight struck ringing across the river from Westminster Abbey like the shuddering moans of lost souls caught in the fog that had begun to collect in the bowl of night and trail like wraiths in and out of the pillars of London Bridge the Spanish Ambassador ordered his men to bring out the prisoner as the tide was beginning to turn and the river which had been so low as to create a beach below the Watergate was now rising swiftly up to the level of the pier.

His watermen took up their positions at the rowlocks and each man lifted his oar ready to dip it in the water on the command of the Cardinal who stood by with the Flemish Ambassador watching helplessly as the Spanish guards carried the inert body of the prisoner to the jetty and laid him gently in the bottom of the boat.

It was too dark to see his face beneath the hood which they had thoughtfully pulled over his head to protect him from the damp mist.

He muttered something but whether it was Flemish or English or some species of dog Latin no-one could tell. It was just the incoherent rambling of a drunk.

"Lay him down gently boys," said the Sergeant-at-Arms in a kindly tone, for he had imbibed generously that evening and was full of good cheer, "you'll get no sense out of him until Evensong tomorrow. That's good English beer for you."

The Spanish guards did not trouble themselves to point out that he had got that way through overindulging in good continental wine. You could not tell the English anything.

Once they were all settled the Cardinal gave the word and the oarsmen dipped their blades into the black murky river. Ripples shone silver and gold in the torchlight as they ran out around the boat and it began to move slowly but surely out into the stream.

The Cardinal watched it as it began to slide swiftly downriver cutting through the shadows like a knife. He watched it until it disappeared and then in his mind's eye there was only the darker shadow of the Tower.

Henry, Richard and Katharine galloped into Greenwich and left their horses at the tavern on the quay which made up one side of a cobbled square in the shadow of the huge Palace. The river ran along the palace and made up the other side of the square.

Ahead of them lay the Scottish caravel *Mary Hamilton* the wind already catching at her shrouds.

The tide had now turned and the river was flowing swiftly. Already the ship had risen so that its gangplank was no longer flat on the jetty but had reached a steep incline.

Sailors had disembarked and were making ready to slip the moorings.

Richard and Katharine turned to bid Henry thanks and farewell.

"No go!" He urged them. "Go! Go! No time for goodbyes. We will drink a toast to each other some other time."

And in some other place he prayed. In Greenwich it was already Christmas morning.

They dashed up the gangplank and onto the deck sighing with relief as they felt the wet boards beneath their feet. They were all but at sea.

As soon as they were on board the sailors loosed the mooring ropes, scurried up the gangplank themselves and began drawing it up after them.

As they did the irresistible pull of the tide began to work against the timbers and the ship heaved herself away from the quay.

Richard and Katharine took up a position on the aft deck from where they could wave Henry farewell.

Their expressions of relief turned to horror as they saw the Portuguese Envoy with his men-at-arms come riding into the square.

Henry was alone in the square. Everyone else was crammed into the tavern ready to raise their glasses to wish the world a Happy Christmas.

He moved to the edge of the quay towards the safety of the *Mary Hamilton* but the ship was already abandoning him creating an ever wider strip of black water between him and his only defence.

Richard and Katharine shouted a warning but there was nothing they could do. With every sweep of the tide the Mary Hamilton moved further and further out of his reach.

The Portuguese dismounted and advanced with drawn swords.

Henry was trapped. He drew his own rapier and stood guard with only a few feet between him and the black icy river.

What could he do? Jump in and swim for it? He thought not. Odds? Four to one. One against four. Not good.

He stepped forward to engage the man nearest to him in a tentative feint.

Odds not good at all.

How would you like it Sir? Italian Style? French? We players are very versatile.

Suddenly like music to his ears sounded the squeal of steel cart-tyres sparking on the cobbles. Shouts rang out and there was the singing of steel, the thud of bone against flesh and the clashing of heads.

The Players had arrived.

The fight was short. This time they had the advantage of surprise as well as an extra man and woman and

Englishmen drawn from the tavern by the noise swiftly threw in their lot against the foreigner.

With four against four, blade against blade, Miles and Elizabeth going round with a cudgel knocking on heads and a scrum of drunken Englishmen throwing their weight on anything that moved it was not long before the Portuguese quartet lay dazed and helpless on the cobbles, disarmed and no longer dangerous.

Buckets of water were thrown over them and they were hauled to their feet with all indignity.

Queen Elizabeth faced up to Sir Pedro Vasc De Cogna, Portuguese Envoy and slipped back her hood so her blonde hair cascaded over her shoulders.

His face was a picture but he was a man of strong nerve and unbounded resource.

He dropped to his knees.

"Majesty!"

She permitted him to kiss her hand.

"Sir Pedro," she greeted him with exquisite courtesy. "Welcome to England."

While they had been otherwise engaged the Mary Hamilton had been steadily drifting out into road. Cheers and hollers had accompanied the arrival of the players and these now reached a crescendo as Richard and Katharine and the Scottish sailors shouted their goodbyes.

"Excuse us," said the Queen politely inviting the Portuguese Ambassador to step aside, "while we make our farewells."

The Players lined up on the quay, put up their swords, joined hands and, as the *Mary Hamilton* was still just visible before she slipped away into the darkness to the open sea, to the great delight of passengers and crew, they took a bow.

The End

Historical Notes

The Princes in the Tower

Of course everyone knows that the two young sons of Edward IV, Edward V and his brother Richard of York, were murdered in the Tower of London if not by, then at the instigation of, their wicked uncle the black-hearted hunch-backed Richard III.

This certainly was the story graphically related to my school party by the Yeoman Warder acting as our guide when we visited the Bloody Tower adding for good measure that the skeletons of the princes had been found buried beneath the flagstones on the ground floor. ("The very flagstones you are standing on boys and girls")

It's a good story but is it true?

The only documentary evidence contemporary with events that suggested the princes were either dead or as good as dead (which is not quite the same thing) in 1483 comes from the letter of the Italian historian Dominic Mancini but they were still alive when Mancini left England before Richard's coronation on 6 July 1483 for although The Greater Chronicle of London reports they were kept under closer guard after the death of Lord Hastings in June 1483 in October of the same year they are recorded as having been seen "shooting and playing in the garden by the Tower" so they were not being kept under very close arrest.

In the same record we are told they "day by day began to be seen more rarely behind the bars and windows" until at length they ceased to appear altogether.

However that does not mean that they were dead.

Mancini's prediction was clearly premature.

It is true that after October 1483 as far as Edward is concerned the trail goes cold.

He must have died quite young, murdered or not, as in 1491 at the start of the rebellion Richard claims the throne in his own right. He could not have done so if his brother was still living at this date.

Edward must therefore have died before the age of 21 but there is not really any firm evidence to say what of, where or at whose hand if not of natural causes. His death remains an unexplained mystery.

But for Richard's survival there is plenty of evidence.

Why is it assumed that he must have died alongside his brother?

While they were both resident at the Tower prior to October 1483 their gradual disappearance might simply be explained by the fact that their uncle had moved them elsewhere.

This would have been a sensible decision on his part because a small rebellious court had grown up around the deposed Edward V and it would be easier to foment conspiracy in London than out in the country.

Nor need they necessarily have continued to be housed together.

There were many good reasons to move the boys out of London. The Tower was not the healthiest of environments. It was usual for the royal households to decamp to the country in the summer months and the royal children were normally housed at one of the outlying palaces, Eltham in Kent or Sheen (Richmond) in Surrey.

As Richard became more confident of his position by late 1483 he might simply have chosen to quietly re-house his nephews somewhere less conspicuous. That they were seen more often indoors in the winter months simply suggests the usual onset of cold weather.

We can certainly say that Edward V was not seen after the spring of 1484 at which date Cardinal Morton declined the offer of pardon Richard had furnished him with by an Act of Parliament passed in January 1484. In April Morton returned without explanation to exile in Flanders and according to the records Henry Medwall went with him as a tutor in his household.

Why did Morton need a tutor?

Did Edward and Richard sail with him?

The reason for the strong inclination of the later historians to accept the conclusion that the two princes were murdered together rests on the discovery in 1673 of the remains of two children in a wooden chest.

These were examined at the time by a number of doctors and then again forensically in 1933.

The identification of these bodies as those of the two princes is decidedly dodgy.

Apologies to the Yeoman Warder but the coffin was not found under the flagstones of the Bloody Tower (so-called because it is believed the princes had their apartments there) but under the foundations of a stone staircase abutting the White Tower which had collapsed.

We do not know how deep the foundations were nor at exactly which depth the coffin was found but if they were supporting a stone staircase it's reasonable to suppose that the coffin was some feet down.

Furthermore if the staircase was part of the original Norman keep it was built in the eleventh century so it's unlikely that any remains found beneath the foundations were fifteenth century in origin.

The White Tower was built on top of the Romano-British Celtic shrine of Bran, the original Raven of the Tower (Bran is Welsh for raven) so any remains under the foundations of the 11th century building are likely to be of the Roman period.

The archaeology does not seem to support the theory that the coffin contained the remains of two renaissance princes.

The forensic evidence is equally unreliable. It was decided, both in 1673 and 1933 that the skeleton of the older child was that of a boy between twelve and thirteen. This corresponds to the age of Edward V in 1483 as he was born in 1470 but there doesn't seem to have been anything else, clothing, jewellery etc to identify him in the coffin. His younger brother was aged ten in 1483 and 'expert witnesses' on both occasions concluded that the younger child's skeleton suggested a child under eight years old. Dental records also confirmed this conclusion.

Modern forensics therefore would be inclined to dismiss the identification on the grounds of insufficient evidence.

The date of this discovery and initial identification should not pass without comment.

The case was a cause célèbre and the boys' remains were re-interred in Westminster Abbey as those of the two princes with great pomp and ceremony despite the dubious nature of the evidence.

In 1673 there was a great debate going on regarding the theory of the Divine Right of Kings. In this year the republicans began a campaign – and indeed introduced an Act of Parliament – to alter the constitution to allow their candidate, the Duke of Monmouth, the illegitimate but crucially Protestant son of Charles II, to succeed instead of his unpopular and Catholic uncle James, Duke of York.

James' only hope was to insist on his bloodline and his legitimacy as the basis of his claim to the throne.

The discovery of the bodies of the 'Princes in the Tower' was a great piece of political propaganda for the Royalists. The tale of the boy-king, divinely appointed and anointed, whose life was snuffed out by the wicked usurper was guaranteed to touch people's hearts.

For this reason we need to be very cautious in dealing with this piece of evidence.

Richard III it has to be said was not anti-nephew per se. He did nothing to harm Edward, Earl of Warwick who survived into the reign of Henry VII until his early twenties although he technically had a better claim to the throne. He was only a toddler at the time and no threat but Richard also nominated his sister's son, John of Lincoln, his only grown up nephew as his heir. Nor did he have any motive to murder the sons of Edward IV as he had had them declared illegitimate by Act of Parliament to remove them legally from the line of succession. There seems little point in going to all that trouble if you are intending to have them murdered.

So there is no firm evidence, documentary or archaeological that suggests Richard of York was murdered with his brother in the Tower even if we accept that Edward V was the victim of such an assassination.

On the other hand what evidence is there that he survived?

The Rebel Prince

Henry Medwall returned to England in 1490 five years after his master John Morton was recalled to serve in the government of Henry VII. Why didn't he come back in 1485?

We have no explanation. We can only point to the coincidence that 1490 is the year in which Richard of York reaches his eighteenth birthday and is no longer in need of a tutor.

In the following year Richard returns to England himself and embarks on his own attempt to regain the throne from Henry Tudor.

Later Tudor history reports that the rebel prince was a mere imposter, the Flemish musician and Plantagenet lookalike Perkin Warbeck.

From contemporary sources it is clear that up to the point of our story the Christmas Feast of 1497 when Warbeck is arrested and taken to the Tower of London no-one was in the slightest doubt that the Pretender was indeed Richard of York.

In fact in the October before the feast there had been a truce and the Mayor of London records that the rebel leader rode in procession with the King without a guard around him and appeared to be on good terms with him. The King not only treated him as his equal he took him to see the Queen his sister who might have been expected to know her own brother.

At no point do any of these people seem to have harboured a suspicion that they were dealing with an imposter.

In late 1497 Henry sought to make a treaty with James IV of Scotland through the Bishop of Durham but he found it impossible to agree terms according to Tudor historian Polydore Vergil

"..because King Henry insisted that Peter Warbeck should be handed over to him..King James specifically urged that he could not hand Peter Warbeck over into the hands of his enemy.. because he was related to the young man by marriage he deemed it dishonourable to deliver him up to his death."

However it was not Perkin Warbeck that they were arguing about. James would not have married his cousin to a Flemish Jewish musician. Polydore Vergil is writing after the arrest of Perkin Warbeck and his identification as the rebel leader. In late 1497 the person Henry wants in custody is the man he believes is Richard Plantagenet. King James will not give him up because he is a royal kinsman. He would not scruple to give up a kinsman who had deceived him and was a commoner to boot.

More interestingly *after* Christmas 1497, in the January of 1498 Henry made a further attempt to make a treaty with Scotland and Polydore Vergil tells us (still assuming that the Pretender and Perkin Warbeck are one and the same person) that "*the most important clause was that James should expel Peter Warbeck from his kingdom.*"

It seems very odd that Henry should make this a deal-breaker because we know that Henry has Peter Warbeck banged up in the Tower. So who is in Scotland that he is keen not to be there?

It can only be that he is referring to Richard of York who has escaped his clutches and found refuge at the Court of James IV.

Henry knows very well that the person he has in custody, Peter Warbeck, is not the man who has led the rebellion against him for six years.

It is almost inconceivable that he would not take some very public steps to punish a commoner and a foreigner who has led a six-year armed rebellion against him and deceived him and his queen under his own nose. But he does nothing. He keeps him under house arrest and lets it be known that the whole rebellion was a hoax much like that of Lambert Simnel with whom he also treated leniently but Lambert Simnel was a boy. Peter Warbeck is a grown man and a foreign national. Why would the King be so gentle with him?

It is true that eventually Peter Warbeck was hanged at the Tower but not for impersonating Prince Richard nor for leading a six year rebellion. He was executed for helping the Earl of Warwick try to escape. Perhaps he was not after all just a simple musician but a Flemish agent?

We are in a world of secret agents. Medwall is not just a chaplain, nor just a playwright, but the confidential secretary of the second most powerful man in England. When Morton died in 1500 having fallen out of the King's favour Medwall promptly resigned his post and as far as the historical record is concerned vanished without a trace.

And Prince Richard?

If he was expelled from Scotland, and Scotland is a big country with a lot of wild backwaters where a man would not be easily found, he probably went back to Flanders but it seems he may have returned to England in his old age.

In the parish register of Eastwell, a small village north of Ashford in Kent, there is an entry dated 1550 which reads as follows: "Rychard Plantagenet was buryed the xxij day of Desember, Anno ut supra" aged 81.

Around this simple fact a whole tradition has grown up suggesting that this refers to an illegitimate son of Richard III but there is no other reference of Richard having a second illegitimate son (he recognised one whose name was John of Gloucester) and most of the stories that have been handed down are of a much later date and the sort of family tales that are inclined to much embroidery along the way.

Richard of York was born in 1473. By 1550 he would be 77 years of age, slightly younger than the 81 years claimed by the parish register for Richard of Eastwell but close enough.

By 1550 Henry VIII was on the throne and the question of the succession, assuming that Richard of York had no surviving sons, had been settled since Henry was also his heir.

It is not impossible that Henry was happy to welcome his uncle home and ready to provide for him a quiet retirement.

However this too is speculation.

The only certain fact we have is that *a* Richard Plantagenet died of very old age in England in 1550.

But if the Richard Plantagenet who was buried at Eastwell was the fugitive prince then he died in his bed.

Not murdered at all.

CPSIA information can be obtained at www.ICGtesting.com
Printed in the USA
LVOW132308130812

294226LV00008B/9/P